LOVE ON THE BOSPHORUS

Tracy Faiers

To order additional copies of this book, contact:
Xlibris
800-056-3182
www.Xlibrispublishing.co.uk
Orders@Xlibrispublishing.co.uk
781227

CHAPTER 1

The bills were due, and once again Lou-Ann had almost no money, almost no job, and soon she would have nowhere to live. She definitely had no husband. Not anymore. The lying cheating bastard. Things were looking very dismal. One could say things were bordering desperate with no way to resolve her problems.

Louise Annabelle Hopkins, previously Masters, had married her college sweetheart, Zak Hopkins, at the tender age of 20. She had meet him at a party whilst still at college, and he turned out to be her one of classmate's handsome older brother. He was her first true love. Her first intimate relationship. She had dated before, but nothing like this.

Zak was a bit of a ladies' man with his film star good looks and swagger. He had been the college heart-throb even after he had finished his education. He would pick his youngest sister up in a flashy car and the girls would all blush and coo. For some reason, he had picked the shy Lou-Ann. Her girlfriends were all envious. She had never understood why he had chosen her. But she was naive and had fallen head over heels in love with him and his charm. What's more, she had trusted him and given him her heart.

The Bastard

The Hopkins family was reasonably well off. They ran a well-established, very respectable haulage and removals company. They had paid for most of the wedding. She had used a small inheritance her grandmother had left her to buy a beautiful wedding dress fit for a princess. The wedding had been held at an old country manor house on a warm, sunny June day. It was a rather grand affair that had gotten out of control with his overbearing mother taking over the arrangements to make it the wedding of the year. However, despite Lou-Ann's reservations, the day was a great success and went off without a hitch.

Zak's parents had also insisted that they give the newly-weds a generous sum of money for deposit on a brand-new, glamorous, two-bed apartment a few minutes' walk from the station. This would make commuting easy for the young couple. Life was sweet. Life was good.

At least for a while.

Lou-Ann wanted to work before settling down to have her own family. She always thought that she would further her education and go to university at some point, but that too looked less likely in her current situation. Meanwhile, she had taken a position in an employment agency in London.

Zak, much to his parents' dismay, had taken a job in a bank in the city rather than helping run the family business or going to university. He guessed he always had that to fall back on. Lou-Ann, on the other hand, had studied international dances. It was a natural progression from the childhood dance lessons her mother had signed her up to at the tender age of three.

It wasn't long before she began to help teach the youngsters tap and ballet. She loved to help out on Saturday mornings when she could. It was a change of pace to her weekday job.

When the honeymoon period was over, cracks in the marriage appeared. Zak started to be delayed at work by last-minute problems or quick beers with the lads from the office, and these became later and later and more frequent. Her father in-law had said it was normal for young lads who worked in the city to let their hair down now and then. She now knew that those beers and last-minute crises were Zak and the office tart getting hot and sweaty under the collar.

Lying, Cheating Bastard

The distraught newly-wed had left Zak and the marital home just after their first Christmas together after a rather compromising photo of him and his tart at the office party had appeared on a social media website. Devastated, Lou-Ann threw a few bags together when he couldn't come up with a good excuse for his behaviour and went to stay at her BFF Jane's tiny flat for a couple of weeks. Then Lou-Ann took up a six-month lease on a small, cramped, one-bed flat on the wrong side of her equally tiny budget.

She also had decided to change jobs. A clean break. The pay was marginally better and nobody would know her situation, which meant less gossip. But now that was all turning out to be as big a mistake as her marriage. Her new company was having some financial difficulties. With job cuts, it meant last in, first out and a two-week notice period. To top it off, her landlord gave her notice to quit with no chance of extending her lease.

Could life get any shittier?

Great! Fantastic! Life sucked big time.

People always say bad things happen in threes. Well, she had no husband, no job, and no home. *Shit, shit, and shit!*

The bastard's wandering dick had really dropped her well and truly in the crapper.

What would she do next?

CHAPTER 2

There was only one more day left at work—and less than two weeks until eviction day and camping out back at Jane's.

Lou-Ann had managed to get a seat on the train halfway home and picked up a freebie evening paper someone had discarded. She turned to the job pages and desperately searched through the ads.

"No. No good. Oh god, this is hopeless," she muttered to herself.

She lifted her head up out of the rag and took a glance round the carriage, wondering who else's life was in the drink. There were people on their mobiles chatting to their loved ones, letting them know what time be picked up from their stops or what time they would be home for dinner. Others were just arranging their social life, and still others were just nodding their heads to their iPods in time to a beat that no one else could hear.

When a city gent opposite smiled at her, she popped her head back into the newspaper and turned the page. In a quiet corner of the page, an advert jumped out at her.

Belly Dancers Wanted
Must have a valid passport.
Immediate travel.
Expenses paid. Short-term contract.
Open auditions Saturday 15 June from 9.30 to 12.
The Royal Hotel, Knightsbridge.
First come, first seen.

Crazy thoughts raced around her brain. It was utter madness but she had to go for it.

What did she have to lose apart from another few weeks of springs in her back on the lovely Jane's sofa? The prospect of free travel and what sounded like a job abroad seemed not a bad option and one she should explore. Hopefully a change for the better.

A wave of excitement washed over her. She had to get this gig. She could do this. Did she have enough confidence to pass herself off as a professional, oriental belly dancer? Zak Hopkins had not only broken her heart; he had shattered her confidence into a million pieces.

"I can do this." A glimmer of hope made her mouth curve up at the corners.

Part of her college course was to study the art of oriental belly dance. Her tutor had said that she would never make a career out of it, but she came out with a pass. Nevertheless, Zak gave her a rare compliment when she had danced for him and said she was quite erotic. But he would say that. The liar. Was anything he said true? Could she really fool these people that she really knew what she was doing? Probably not, but she had to try anyway.

The word *rusty* swirled around her head as the train pulled into her stop.

The kettle was boiling, and a value spaghetti meal in her microwave, the only thing she had taken from her marital home, was set for seven minutes. The realization of what she was going to do hit her. Today was Thursday, and that gave her a short time to rehearse.

"I can't believe I am actually contemplating this." escaped from her lips.

Jane was due to come around to her apartment the next evening, but she would have to put her off.

After the kettle clicked off, Lou-Ann went to make a coffee, but she spotted three quarters of a bottle of cheap Merlot. She decided this would be a better idea than the coffee. With a bit of Dutch courage, she poured herself a healthy-sized glass of the ruby-coloured liquid and took a large gulp.

Then she went to her small but neatly arranged bedroom. In the back of her closet was an old, battered, navy suitcase filled with her college dance costumes and memorabilia. She opened the case.

On the top of everything were some DVDs, including one marked, "End of Year Show. "Perfect," she said to herself.

She took the shiny disc out of its case and marched back to the lounge, where she turned on the television and DVD player and pressed play. The microwave pinged, indicating that her meal was cooked.

After taking another slurp, she topped her glass up with the Merlot and took her meal and wine to the sofa, where she got comfy and watched the concert.

The good old days, she thought.

There were all sorts of acts. Singers, Russian dancers, a group of lads trying to do the Greek Zorba dance. One of the dancers leaped in the air and fell on his backside, which in turn started the cast giggling. It was so bad it was funny.

A group of the finest ballet dancers recreated a scene from *Swan Lake*. She knew her oriental showcase was coming up soon so she ran to the kitchen to put the plastic container in the bin and the cutlery in the sink. And to drink yet another gulp of wine. The effect of the alcohol was now spreading through her, giving her a warm, fuzzy feeling and a little bravado. It felt good to reminisce.

When she heard the intro, she ran back and paused the concert. Feeling even braver, she went back to the battered suitcase in her bedroom and rummaged through until she found her old costume. It consisted of a push up bra covered in red chiffon and hundreds of hand sown sequins bought cheap from the local market and a pair of black oversized harem pants and a red coin belt.

Before she knew it, her office clothes were strewn on the floor as she wondered if it would still fit her slender body

"I must have a screw loose if I think I can pull this off." She said as if she was talking to someone in the room with her. She knew what Jane would say. "You need your head testing girly." Jane would support her any way. She pulled on the outfit and smiled as it fitted her perfectly formed body and checked herself out in the mirror. "Not bad, not bad at all." She smiled again please with herself. She had been trying to keep herself fit with a Zumba DVD as her gym membership was now far too costly.

She took another gulp of the more you drink the better it tastes red liquid.

Standing back in front of the television, she depressed the pause button and restarted the concert. The intoxicating sound of Arabic music washed over her like sensual wave. It took her by surprise. She wondered how much of the routine she would remember. Her hips started to sway trying to mirror the image on the screen. 30 seconds later and six beats behind Lou-Ann yelled at herself

"I'm hopeless. Who am I trying to kid? Rusty is not the word for it. Come on hips don't let me down, get it together. Another swig of this should help." She drew in a big breath. "Relax girly, let the music do its thing."

This time with another bigger deeper breath she started to move with the backbeat of the drums gently undulating her hips into figures of eights followed by hip drops and Arabs. "Much better!" she breathed out a sigh of relief. "Let's rewind and start again. Practice makes perfect." She started to repeat the process over again. Her muscle memory kicked in and she began to relaxed more and more with each step. Each time she repeated the dance her movements became smoother and began to increase speed and added some turns. The music begun to crescendo, indicting the piece was coming to an end. A few final twirls around the tiny floor she collided with the shabby two setter and collapsed laughing out loud.

"Oh, what will they think on Saturday?" Feeling a bit giddy with a heady mix of cheap wine and twirling around "let's do this thing, at least I can laugh at myself". She picked up her wine glass for last sip but her head was still spinning, she decided to she would have an early night ready for her last day at work and her last chance to practice in the evening. Lou-Ann laid her costume over the chair and put the suitcase in the corner, drew the curtains and climbed on her bed pulling on her favourite night shirt then lay down. Sleep came fast and left her dreaming of hope and a better future.

CHAPTER 3

The sun crept around the corner of the curtain sneaking in a small ray of hope as she opened her eyes. There's that word again. Hope.

Hoping she could bluff her way her way into the job. Hoping that she would be able to cope with the audition without messing up and freaking out. Hoping things could only get better. She at least deserved that much. This situation was that bastard's fault and not of her doing.

"Oh, my head" she mumbled as she rolled out of her bed. "Last day kiddo. Let's go to it." Two pain killers and twenty-five minutes later she was at the station heading into work for last time. She was going to have to put Jane off this evening. The only trouble was she hated not telling her why as Jane always had a way of dragging the truth out of her. A short text later she had developed a migraine would only be a small fib. After all she had woken up with a headache in the morning.

Lou-Ann and Jane had been friends for ever with hardly a cross word said between then. They were joined at the hip all through school only falling out over a boy, who later turned out not even to like girls. They still often laughed over it now.

She would tell her friend after the audition so they could laugh about that too.

The day dragged by slowly and Lou-Anne crept out of the office a little before five with no fuss just clutched a small bunch of flowers from the 2 ladies she has sat next to. She went home and practice as much as she could and hoped that would suffice. She put her old iPod shuffle on charge as it had some Arabic tracks on it. She hoped on her journey the next day the music would inspire her.

Having tapped her oyster card she found herself on the underground heading towards Knights Bridge carrying a pretty tote bag over her arm that contained her costume. Nerves were creeping up on her making her stomach churn. Be calm, stay calm, I am calm was the mantra she repeated to herself. She still couldn't quite believe that she was going through with this hair brained scheme.

It was a warm sunny morning when she excited the tube station. She crossed the road and head towards the hotel. It was 8.50am. She was hoping that there weren't going to be too many people in front of her. Now she was at the venue all she wanted to get it over and done with. The sooner the better.

She was directed to the first-floor conference rooms and shown were to change. When she was ready Lou-Ann waited in an adjoining room. There were several beautiful girls there already including a blonde leggy Russian who had already changed into an ornate bejewelled costume. *Must her cost her a pretty penny* she thought. Obviously a professional. Her nerves bubbled to the surface. She hoped her face would not give her away. She just needed to stay calm for just a little while longer and let fate deal it's hand.

It seemed nobody knew what it was exactly what the audition was for but it had been an opportunity not to be missed. Everyone was given a short questionnaire. She decided that she would use her maiden name, Masters. After all that was what was on her passport. Three other girls had arrived after her. She was told she would be number four by a silvery grey-haired man who was dressed in a smart suit. 9.30 arrived and the first act was called. Twin sisters, a novelty double act. They were so alike she wondered if they ever played tricks on people. They seemed to take forever. Eventually they exited the room looking miserable. She guessed they hadn't got the job. They leggy blonde in her over jewelled outfit went next. That was the longest fifteen minutes of her life. At one point she thought she was going to puke when her stomach churned violently.

"Please Miss, this way. They are waiting for you." The voice made her jolt and her knees shake. She decided she needed a scarf. This would give her something to hide behind. Hide her anxiety.

Lou-Ann spotted another girl with a gorgeous multi coloured silk scarf and asked if she could borrow it.

"Of course." she replied begrudgingly. Another rotund girl mouthed good luck to her.

"Miss, when you are ready please." The suited man said impatiently.

She had scooped up her wayward hair into a genie style ponytail on the top of her head which swayed as she walked into the room trailing the scarf behind her in one hand not having the time to hide behind it and wishing she had a glass of that magical Merlot in the other for some Dutch courage.

Her heart started to bang loudly against her chest. She could have sworn that everyone else in the building could have heard it.

Breathe, girly breathe.

She did her best to swallow her fears and held her head up high and glanced around the room briefly to familiarise herself with the space. The walls were whitewashed with gilded fleur de lice cornices and several oil paintings on the walls. The only furniture was a table and two chairs and a large lattice work folding screen. On the chairs sat the same well-dressed man and an a lady who was in her late 30's. She was stunning with beautiful dark eyes made up like an Egyptian goddess and dark tumbling hair. Lou-Ann spotted her long immaculately manicured nails splayed across the table which made her squeeze her own fingers into her palms shamefully. Regular manicures were also something else that had fallen by the wayside.

GOD. She hated auditions. They always made her feel sick and go wobbly at the knees. That was the reason she never wanted to dance professional but today was different. She had to look and act the part even in her home-made costume. The scarf that she had purloined didn't really go with her outfit but it would have to suffice.

Suddenly she wished she knew what she was going to dance to and hope it would be familiar.

"Are you ready my dear?" The Egyptian eyed woman spoke softly to her as if sensed her nerves. Lou-Ann nodded. She placed herself gracefully in the middle of the floor with her feet slightly turned out one in front of the other then scooped up the scarf and hid inside it. Her stomach churned and she hoped they didn't hear it. She swallowed hard. The music started thankfully it sounded vaguely familiar though at that moment in time she couldn't remember any of the rhythms.

She started to move the scarf around in swirling patterns at first to build her confidence. She pulled the veil back up to her face. She then started to move her hips in figures of eights in time to the drum beat. Grapevine to the left sweeping one arm with the veil the other side. She gave a little shimmy then decided to turn. Her foot suddenly got tangled in her damn oversized pantaloons. The floor came crashing quickly towards her landing on one side with a small thud.

"Oh, holy hell!" The words just blurted out. She wanted the ground to open up and swallow her whole. Too embarrassed to look up at the people at the table who had an 'ouch' look on their faces. The music was paused. Picking herself up from the floor she turned to head for the door. Tears threatened.

From behind the screen she heard a small girly giggle. But what stopped her in her tracks, it was the smooth male voice that whispered loudly.

"Shush little one, it's rude to laugh at people." A girl's voice responded.

"I like her Pappa, she's funny." And with that she ran from behind the screen and yelled "Please do not leave." The cute little girl was standing next to her looking up into face with a huge irresistible smile and big brown eyes. She had to be about five or six with tussled black curls around her olive-skinned face. "Are you OK lady? Are you hurt?"

"I'm fine honey, only my pride. I think my bottoms going to be sore though." The child put her hands to her face and giggled. A man came alongside her, presumably her father. He was tall, dark and bloody handsome. Her heart flipped.

"I apologise for the secrecy Miss Masters. I am Ahmet Bahar and this is my daughter, Halise. She can be very distracting. She wasn't supposed to be here today but the arrangements I made for care failed to appear and so the rest you know." He held out his hand "Come Miss, start again." She put her fingers in his palm as he led her back to the centre of the room, his dark sexy eyes never leaving hers. Her heart flipped again. "Would you like a different piece of music? Do you have a favourite?"

"Yes, Sir I do. Do you have Shik shak shok?" She knew it was now or never. Her immediate future depended on getting right this time.

Mr Bahar looked at the Egyptian looking lady.

"I think we can manage that don't you Madame Massari?" She pressed a few buttons on her shiny laptop.

Madame Massari nodded to Lou-Ann "Are you ready this time? Relax and enjoy, Miss Masters."

"Yes, yes I'm ready." As ready as she was going to be. Hope and courage shot through like something had woken up inside her.

Mr sexy eyes and his daughter moved to the side of the room. Halise smiled a big smile at her then at her father. The music began once more and the familiar music relaxed her. She inhaled deeply. Take two. Her feet lightly gliding over the wooden floor as moved hypnotically around the room. Her hips swaying and rotating, her breast rising and falling breathlessly to the exotic music. Her heart and soul poured out into the dance. She was totally oblivious to his hot sexy eyes following her every step. Her every scintillating move. Moves she didn't realise she even knew. His daughter standing next to him, watcher her with delight. It was like a spell was being cast. No laughter, only exotic music with the soft sound of her bare feet brushing the floor and the jingle of her coin belt as she shimmied.

As the music came to the it's end, she realized he was watching her face. The hope that had grown in the beginning begun to fade and die. How could she even stand a chance against the leggy Russian in all her finery? She suddenly felt very foolish. Lou-Anne gathered herself together and picked up the borrowed scarf. Who am I kidding? What's the point of carrying on this façade? she thought and started heading for the door. Halise tugged on her father's suite jacket and whispered something in his ear.

"Miss Masters please wait." Ahmet said with a tone of urgency. She turned to face them. "It seems my daughter thinks you have hidden talents and has taken a shine to. Please would you wait till the end?"

He also found her somewhat amusing. Even arousing. He admired her courage.

"Yes sir, of course I will." She winked at Halise before she skipped to the door with amazement. She felt his eyes watch her all the way to the door.

She breathed a sigh of relief that it was over and passed back the scarf with a polite thank you trying not giving anything a way. She was still a little bewildered by his reaction to her. She was sure he would send her home with a 'not what we are looking for today and a thanks for coming anyway.'

At just gone twelve pm after all the others had left disappointed. That just left Lou-Ann and the Russian in the waiting area awaiting their instructions. The leggy blonde had introduced herself as Claudia Bolshov. She seemed to think she was far superior and looked down her nose at everyone. The door opened and the smart suited man came over to them and gave them some papers to sign. "I am Osman, Mr Bahar's personal assistant, please read." He informed that there travel arrangements would be made for Tuesday to fly to Istanbul and their tickets would be waiting for them at the airport. They were to be given a reasonable sized advance on arrival and the rest at the end of the job which was the equivalent of about £1200. Not bad she thought, in fact it was more than she thought it would be.

She stared at the papers in utter disbelief. Surely there were better candidates than her. It had seemed obvious that Claudia would be chosen from the beginning. Lou-Ann's lack of self-confidence came creeping back. It was hard to concentrate on the content of the papers as Ahmet's eyes seemed leap of the paper instead of words. "Concentrate girly, he has no interest in you. You are lowly dancer with a contract to sign. Simple." She muttered under her breath. Besides, Jane's sofa would still be there on her return along with Jane's everlasting friendship so what had she got loose. So, with that she gave up trying to read it all and signed on the dotted line before she had time to change her mind or for them to reconsider.

"ok, done" handed the paper back to Osman. He reminded of Omar Sherif, with his silvery salt and pepper wavy hair and had an air of sophistication about him.

She was off to Istanbul for a new adventure.

Ahmet Bahar had been in London for business. He came from a very long line of Bahar's that were renowned for their fine bespoke jewellery. Their heritage was said to go as far back as the great Sultan's of the old city of Constantinople. They dealt in the finest diamond and precious gem stones from around the world, designing and making bespoke jewellery for their special customers and exclusive limited editions for high end department stores in London, Paris and New York.

Aken, Ahmet's older brother by two years had branched out and owned a boutique hotel and his younger brother, Bugra or Bobby as everyone close called him, had just finished his national service. He was set to go into the family business too. Probably more into the financial side of things as he had studied to be an accountant at university. After their fathers impending retirement, they would all take control of the business.

A shopping trip to Harrod's was part of the agenda. He intended to find his farther an appropriate gift for his birthday. But what do you buy for a man who could buy whatever he wanted and not forgetting little Halise. He also wanted to find her a lovely suitable dress for the celebrations.

There was to be a spectacular party for his father with international dancers performing at the majestic affair. He had the idea of an audition to see if he could some additional talent to add to some flavour the occasion.

Money was no object. The Bahar men were used to getting what they desired and at any cost and when they wanted it. Except when it came to his daughter. She melted his heart and caved at most of her demands even at such a tender age of five and a half. It was her influence that had led to the hiring of the pretty girl in the baggy black harem pants even though her dancing skills were not up to scratch and defiantly not up to Madame Massri's usual standard. Admittedly had fallen a little for her and her shyness and tenacity. He had seen something in her too! But what only time would tell.

Despite Madame Jasmine Massri's doubts, he had hired her anyway. He thought she was worth the risk. When he looked into her eyes, they stirred him in a way that had long been forgotten. Not since before the death of his wife.

On the way home Lou-Anne decided to call Jane and tell her that she wouldn't need to take her offer up of her trusty sofa after all. At least not for a while.

"That's fantastic news Annie, congratulations." Jane was excited for her though wary. "Just be careful of those greasy Turks." They both giggled. Jane continued "Make sure you drink plenty of water, it will be really hot out there."

"Yes, Mother dear." She retorted. Jane continued

"Ooohh, don't forget to get a good sun cream. You know how you burn as soon as you look at the sun." They giggled again.

"I will I promise."

"I will come and help you pack tomorrow and you can fill me in on the details. I'll ring my Dad later and see if you can store some stuff in his loft." Lou-Anne could hear Jane choke back the tears on the other end of phone. That made her want to cry too. She sniffed and brushed away a tear. She was glad Jane was pleased for her and after all she was only going to be away for three and half to four weeks. Not exactly going to be away for a life time.

When she got home, she would have to call her own father. She told him she was going travelling in Turkey with a friend for a month so as not to worry him too much. Though like most parents he would worry about his daughter traveling in a foreign land, alone or otherwise, but he wished her a good luck, told her to stay safe and have a good time.

"Watch out for those greasy Turks." She laughed.

"That's exactly what Jane said. I promise Dad."

"Good girl. Make sure you send a post card or two. When you get home, you must visit. Marsha will be as fat as a whale with your baby brother. Ouch!!" She heard Marsha putting her dad in his place with a dig in the ribs. So far, she had not bothered him to much with her problems. She had not wanted to worry him. Financially he was barely making ends meet himself with her stepmother. Her own mother had died of cancer when she was 9 after a long illness.

That's why her dancing has always been so important to her. Her father had met Marsha around the same time Lou-Ann met Zak and it became clear very early on their relationship that it was more than friendship. Marsha too had been widowed.

It had been nice for Lou-Ann to have a mother figure around though Marsha had never had any children of her own. They would go on the regular shopping trips and lunch together now and then. When her father lost his job they decided to sell up and moved to west country thinking that Lou-Ann now had a safe enough life style for them not to have be around and start their own new life. Which now was literally what had happened. At 49 and 44 they were about to become parents. Shock had not been the word. Marsha had been told she would probably never have children from a young age.

Once everyone had got used to the idea, they were all pleased as punch. Lou-Ann was finally going to have a brother she had always craved.

CHAPTER 4

Tuesday came a round fast. Her things had been safely stored in Jane's father's loft and garage. Jane had given her a small bag and had given her strict instructions not to open until she was on the plane. Once seated Loo-Ann peered into the bag, it contained a guidebook of Istanbul and two hundred and fifty Turkish lira with a bright pink post-it-note stuck on the top saying just in case.

"Oh Jane!" She said as she clawed back the tears. Thank god for her trusted friend.

Before she knew it, she had landed and cleared customs. She'd found a trolley to put her bags on and headed for the exit. She had expected to have to haggle with a local taxi driver but to her relief she saw a familiar face dressed in his usual smart suit with Miss Masters written on a board. It was Osman, Mr Bahar's confidant and driver. She felt her heart sank a little as she realized she was disappointed that it wasn't Mr sexy eyes himself standing there to greet her. But the unexpected lift was appreciated all the same.

As Osman moved to greet her, she saw the little girl clutching his other hand. Lou-Ann smiled at Halise. Yet another surprise. The girl smiled the biggest, cheesiest grin she could manage. She could barely contain her excitement to see Lou-Ann.

She felt something maternal stir inside her as Halise broke free and ran towards her with arms outstretched as if she was greeting a long-lost friend or relative. Halise's overly enthusiastic greeting took her aback.

"I begged my Pappa for me to meet and he said no and I asked again and again till he said yes and then he said Uncle Osman can come get you because he didn't need him today and as long as I was good I could come to get you and I promised that" she continued to blurt out virtually in one breath.

Lou-Ann interrupted her

"Slow down, slow down." She bent down a kissed the top of her head. "Well I'm very glad that you did young lady." She then looked to Osman "Thank you Osman, I am so very grateful."

"Her father spoils her Miss Masters but I am happy to be of service too you. Your bags please Miss."

With that Osman led the way. Halise held Lou-Ann's hand as tight as she could and skipped all the way to the car park. Osman got his keys from his pocket and pressed the button. A beautiful bright red shiny BMW bleeped.

Bags safely stowed and seat belt on they headed towards the city. The evening air was thick and sticky, she was glad the vehicle had air conditioning. The traffic got even denser the closer they got to the city. The skyline was amazing there appeared to be hundreds of minarets poking out from the hills reaching up to the sky.

Before long they pulled up outside a stunning white stoned building. It was the hotel where she would be staying. Halise's constant chatter had made the journey seam shorter. How wonderful to be able to speak a different language perfectly at such a young age. She wished she had paid more attention in her language classes when she was a school.

Osman opened the car door for her as if she was royalty. He gathered up her bags from the boot of the car and gave them to the young bell hop that had magically appeared. The young chap looked like he would snap in half if lifted anything heavier than a fluffy pillow. She gave Halise a hug before she exited the car.

"Will I see you soon?" Halise chirped.

"I hope so little one. I hope so."

Osman had already explained that she would receive her schedule tomorrow and suggested she rested that evening and got adjusted to the heat. She thanked him once again and waved as they set off. She followed the skinny bell hop and checked in.

The white marble interior felt cool compared to the sticky air outside. Gilded framed mirrors had been strategically placed to make the space feel larger and even more luxurious. Ceiling fans danced around in circles pushing the air around the foyer. A large lush red crushed velvet couch was placed alongside the check-in desk. Two tall vases were filled with long stemmed dark pink lilies either side of the plush sofa, which stood upon glass tables that looked like they had dragon's feet attached to them. The sweet scent of the floral display perfumed the air.

Paperwork completed and keys in hand she followed the skinny boy to the lift.

Safely ensconced in her hotel room, which was far superior to anything she could have imagined, she put her handbag on the huge bed. The bell hop had managed to get her bags to her room without snapping in half. Lou-Ann tipped him a few Lyra and he seemed happy as he nodded and thanked her. She sat next to her bag on the end of the bed and suddenly felt overwhelmed by everything. That morning she was homeless in London. The same evening she was in a fabulous boutique hotel with no one to share it with. Then there was the little girl, she had stolen a small piece of her heart.

As promised, she pinged a text to father and to Jane letting them know of her safe arrival at her destination and that all was well. She promised to stay in touch when possible.

Lou-Ann decided that she would unpack her things straight away and get herself organised. She hung up her clothes in the wardrobe, toiletries neatly displayed in the bathroom and placed her hairbrush and a small bottle of perfume on the dressing table. She noticed there was a hotel guide, 2 bottles of complementary water one still, one sparkling. That was accompanied by pen and paper and a post card depicting the hotel and few of the well-known sites.

"I think I'll send that to Jane. She would like that. I'll find a different one for Dad and Marsha."

With everything now in its rightful place, she decided to shower. She soaped up with the lush citrus lather and washed away all her troubles and looked forward to the next few weeks and the financial reward at the end of it.

Wrapped up the finest, largest white fluffy towels you can imagine an exhausted Lou-Ann called room service then laid on the bed.

The next morning, she awoke refreshed but tangled in the crisp white sheets and stretched her arms out and survey her unfamiliar surroundings almost forgetting where she was. She was thankful that she had hung the contents of bag already so the creases had dropped out overnight. She grasped a pair of white linen trousers and a pretty pink t-shirt, grabbed her undies and laid them on the bed. She took another quick shower and dressed and wondered down to breakfast clutching the little guidebook that Jane a bought her.

"Merhaba, good morning Miss, please take a seat." An elderly waiter pointed to a table neatly laid with white linen and silver cutlery and condiments. "Yes Miss. Please I am Enza, you need anything, you ask me OK." With a nod of the head then continued to take her breakfast order. She had a range of things from the menu including scrambled eggs, croissants and some mixed fruits. She hadn't realized how hungry she was until she started eating. Though well rested the hearty meal would keep her on her toes whilst she ventured out after breakfast.

"Excuse me Enza, could you show me were on my map and please call me Lou-Ann." After a second or two he pointed to an area to an area on the fold up map of her guidebook.

"Here Miss." She took her pen a put a cross to mark the position of the hotel and nodded at him with appreciation. "Hos geldines Miss."

Maybe he didn't feel comfortable using her given name so she didn't bother to correct him. She placed the guidebook safely in her bag and zipped it up tight. At reception she asked if anything had been left for her. The pretty young girl shook her head and said she would let her know if anything arrived later in the day. It suddenly occurred that she hadn't yet seen the leggy blonde in her hotel but she assumed that she had just not crossed paths yet. Then put the thought away.

The heat of the day hit her as stepped out the hotel. The sun was already high in the sky and it wasn't quit even 11 yet. The heat would be something she would have to adjust to over the next few weeks. By the time she had been walking for only ten minutes she had already drank half of the bottle of water she had taken from the room and wished she has brought the other.

She wondered around for a while around for a while then Lou-Ann stopped at a street vendor to replenish her empty water bottle for a freezing cold new one and an ice-cream, a strawberry cheesecake in a waffle cone which was her favourite. After looking in a few of the local shops that were very expensive filled beautiful designer clothes she could never afford, it became apparent that the area she was staying was not in the touristic part of the city but an upmarket cosmopolitan neighbourhood. Hot and bothered she meandered back the hotel.

It was gone 1.45 before she returned and hadn't realized she had been gone so long. Hot and sticky she glanced at the reception desk and headed in that direction.

"Miss Masters, a call came for you from Mr Bahar. His driver will be here to collect you at 3.30."

A waft of the pink lilies tickled her nose as she scanned the girls name badge. "Thank you Deani."

Excited and ready before time she waited in the lobby. There had been enough time for her to rest for a while and smarten up a little before then. Her face was a little pink from the mornings walk. She wished she bought that's sunscreen she promised Jane. Tomorrow she would have to buy a decent cream and a hat otherwise she would be as red as the car she was about to take a ride in.

Her excitement grew as she waited by the desk where she had checked in the previous day. She was thinking about Ahmet's dark sexy eyes. It was having quite an effect on her. Osman appeared and disturbed her daydreaming.

"Hope you are well Miss Masters?"

"Yes Osman, I am very well thanks."

As before, Osman led her to the car and opened the door. "I think young Halise will be pleased to see you Miss Masters."

It was a short drive to an even more affluent part of city. Huge pine trees obscured the large beautiful homes that hid behind them. Osman pulled of the main road and headed up a private track that lead to a gated driveway. With a click of a button the large ornate gates swiftly flung open that led up the Bahar's residence. Her jaw hit the floor and a 'WOW' escaped her lips. She saw Osman smile at her reaction. It was like something from a film. Even Zak's family didn't live in such grandeur. She felt like was a princess arriving at a castle.

There was a white two storey ranch style building with terracotta roof tiles, large Romanesque columns stood century. The lawn was a lush green with sweet smelling grass. The car pulled up between two of the columns next to two ornate carved wooden doors. Either side of heavy doors stood two hip height vases decorating the entrance. They were blue mosaic filled with trailing ivy and little pink flowers poking their heads out reaching for the scorching sun.

The door opened is if by magic. There stood a well-kept older lady wearing an apron.

"This is my wife, Zita." Osman explained "She understands some English but does not speak it so well." The two women smiled warmly at each. Zita held out her arm and beckoned Lou-Ann to follow her.

"Merhaba! Come, please." Lou-Ann followed her through the doors and Zita pointed to side room in the hallway. "Sit, sit. Please wait here." The she disappeared again.

It was cool in here. The wall where clad with finest white flecked marble with black and white squares on the floor. Two chairs and a bench furnished the room. Covering some of the floor tiles was a gorgeous intricately patterned Turkish rug in rich reds and golds. On the furniture were cushions that complemented the rug. On the wall there was a picture of a stunning young woman holding a small child. Either side there were tall crystal glasses filled with perfumed white roses.

Zita came back into the room clutching a silver tray with two small glasses and an ornate silver tea pot.

"Apple tea? Is good for you. You drink, yes?" Zita proceeded to pour the fragrant liquid into one of the glasses. "Mr Bahar he come soon. Ok?"

"Ok. That's very kind. Thank-you Zita."

"Hos geldines canim." With that Zita scurried of again.

Lou-Ann sat with her tea and stared at photo of the mother and a child. She couldn't help but wonder who she was.

"Good afternoon Miss Masters." He smiled. "Glad you could join us."

He had made her jump with surprise nearly spilling her tea as she hadn't heard him enter the room. "I am sorry. I did not mean to startle you. I was caught up on the telephone to New York."

She tried desperately not to look in his black oily eyes. They were eyes that you could fall into and never want to leave. He was were khaki trousers with a cream loose fitting linen shirt. He looked as sexy as hell, but to late their eyes had locked. She felt a little bolt of lightning hit her deep inside. She blushed. Feeling just a bit embarrassed she looked back at the picture on the wall as it seemed to be a safe place to avert her eyes.

"My wife!" Ahmet offered.

"Oh. OOOHHH." Lou-Ann hadn't even given any thought to his marital status.

"She died three years ago in a car accident. We keep this room so Halise can remember her mother and for her to know that her mother loved her. This was one of her favourite rooms in the house."

A tear trickled down her check. She knew what it was like to grow up without a mother. "I am so sorry. Poor little Halise." Were the only words she could muster. She felt a little guilty for having inappropriate thoughts about him. After all this was a business arrangement and she would have to keep her thoughts in check. Though strange undeniable things happened to her body when he was close to her.

"Please" He put his hand on her shoulder "Please it is ok. We all miss her so much but we manage." With the other hand he wiped the tear away with his finger. He released her and picked up the silver tray. "I didn't mean to upset you."

"It just was the thought of Halise growing up without her Mother. I know what that's like." She followed him like a little lost dog back into the hallway which split the house in half. They approached a large patio door and stepped in the garden. A large paved area ran across the back the house. To her left there was an arbour with Russian vines growing making shade from the sun. The whole place was spectacular. She took a seat in the shadiest part of the arbour and tried not to stop her mouth popping open with awe.

"I hope your hotel room is sufficiently comfortable for you. Have you settled in ok Miss Masters?"

"It is lovely, very much like your home. It's much more than I was expecting and please call me Lou-Ann." She went on to explain that waiter at breakfast was very kind and very helpful to her and that to her surprise the skinny bell boy had managed to lift her case without folding in half.

"I am very glad to hear it Lou-Ann. My older brother will be pleased. He owns the hotel you are staying in. He takes things quite personally when his guest are not happy" He smiled at her "and if I am to call you Lou-Ann you must call me Ahmet." he insisted "I have asked you here today as you have caused me a bit of a conundrum and it concerns Halise." Lou-Ann looked at him a bit confused after all she hardly knew the girl.

"How can I help?" she offered curiously.

"My daughter is smitten with you and refusing to go to the summer house with her cousins, grandparents and some other members of the family. We have a holiday home in Kusadasi. It was only going to be short beak this year anyway because of my father's party." He gleefully raised an eyebrow "I think you have cast a spell on her." When in fact he knew it was himself her spell had actually befallen upon.

They both looked at each other and laughed a little. Her thoughts mirrored his own. She hoped she wasn't going to blush again.

"I wondered if you would be so kind "He begun again "to help with her care whilst you are here. I will reimburse you for your time. Osman will drive you whenever I do not need him. I will also set up an account with a taxi company so you will not have to worry about getting around the city.

"What about rehearsals?"

"Well we can schedule everything around them and I am sure I can rearrange some of my meetings. Zita will be around too. Halise is a bit to boisterous for her to have her for a long time."

"Your daughter is an absolute delight; I would be happy to have her." *And I will get to see more of you* she thought sneakily. After all she had come her to work and make some cash and the extra monies would be useful upon her return to England.

"Excellent. As for rehearsals they have been delayed for a few days. Madame Massari had to fly home from London on Saturday evening for a family emergency."

"I hope that everything is going to be ok?"

"Yes, I understand things are fine, as is Madam Massari. She should be back for rehearsals to start Monday so you have a few days free time to adjust to the heat and enjoy the delights of our beautiful city."

They both turned at the same time when they heard footsteps running on the patio.

"Pappa, Pappa." Halise ran to her father without stretched arms and he stood to greet her. Ahmet lifted her high into the air and whirled her around. Both father and daughter smiled with delight. He lowered her back to the ground and her feet had barely touched the floor for more than a second when she rushed over to Lou-Ann and threw her arms round her with as much gusto as she had greeted her father. She automatically hugged the child back.

Halise went back to her father and whispered something loudly in Turkish into his ear.

"Why don't you ask her yourself Halise?"

"Please will you stay for supper, Pappa does not mind and Zita's food is yummy and Pappa can get you some nice wine." Halise gave her look she could not or dare not refuse.

"Ok, ok I will stay for dinner little miss. As long as it is not too much trouble."

"Well that seems to settle that. Halise go find Zita and tell her that we have a special guest for dinner." Halise skipped of happily to find Zita.

Ahmet smiled seeing his daughter happy. "You didn't not need much persuading, did you?"

"How can I refuse that angelic little face? Besides, I have no other plans for this evening. She is very beautiful Ahmet. She looks like her mother."

"She is very much like her mother in more ways than one. Come I will show you the rest of the garden." Ahmet held out his hand to her and she gently placed her hand in his for what seemed the longest few seconds.

He felt it and she felt it. A spark had ignited between them. A deep sensual stirring. Something he hadn't felt for three long years. His groin twitched. He had to remind himself that this was a professional relationship and nothing else.

Halise had seen them hold hands for those few seconds. It made her giggle. She ran back out to the garden and ran between them and held their hands. From behind you have thought they were a family.

The back of the garden was high up on a cliff top. They stopped and watched the Bosphorus worm its way into the city. Just like this little family was worming its way into her heart.

CHAPTER 5

They sat in the cool of the dining room around one end of a large table. Zita cooked one of Halise's favourites. it was a local chicken dish, almost like a mild curry with almonds and raisins but not like anything she had had before. She had also prepared several other dishes, all were sensational. Halise had been right, Zita certainly new how to cook. It was a feast fit for kings. There was so much food Lou-Ann thought Zita had cooked everything in the cupboards.

Ahmet opened a bottle of his finest red wine, a special reserve that he had been saving. Now seemed to be that perfect occasion. It complemented the meal perfectly. Lou-Ann was careful not to drink too much too quickly. She did not want to embarrass herself.

After the main meal was over Ahmet announced to Halise that Lou-Ann would going help out with her care. She squealed with delight and excitement. She chatted not stop as usual and they discussed some things that Lou-Ann might want to see or where she could take Halise out for a treat.

"Saturday we could go to the Grand Bazaar." Ahmet declared "A must for any tourist. It will be fun." He looked straight at Lou-Ann with a smile.

"That would be wonderful." She said trying to avoid looking directly into his eyes.

Halise had seen the way her father had looked at Lou-Ann. She started to giggle. Then for no apparent reason they all joined in. A large serving of laughter and ice cream was dished up for dessert.

After the beautiful noise had subsided and the ice cream had vanished it was time for the young one to go to bed.

"Oh! Pappa do I have to go right now?" Halise protested screwing up her little face.

"Yes, you do. Bed. Now." He answered her firmly.

Halise looked across to Lou-Ann.

"Can Lou-Ann take me to bed Pleeeease!"

Both Halise and Ahmet looked at her in expectation.

"Of course I will take you. Say good night to your father then you can show me your room. I bet it's pink?" Halise shook her head in agreement. Putting her to bed just seemed a natural thing to do.

The room was full of pink and cream frills. The mini four poster bed and the curtains were draped in pinks and creams. The bed was filled with soft toys.

"Wow! This is amazing."

Halise went to clean her teeth and changed into her pink spotty cotton pyjamas and headed for her princess bed.

"My mummy did this for me just before she went to heaven." She was quite matter of fact about it. Her words chocked Lou-Ann. She knew what it was like not to have a mother tuck you in at night.

"Well she did a fantastic job for her little girl." She patted the bed. "Come on hop in." she kissed her forehead "sleep tight see you soon. Night night little one."

"Iyi geceler." Halise rolled over clutching her favourite teddy bear which took pride of place on the pillows.

As she turned and headed for the door her heart jumped into her mouth for the second time today. Ahmet was leaning against to door frame he was smiling at her. He knew had startled her and mouthed a sorry.

"I am beginning to think that my daughter was right. You are a natural Miss Master." He whispered as they headed for the staircase. "I have enjoyed this evening very much askim."

"So have I. I should go. I will look forward to Saturday."

They reach the bottom of the stairs

"Me too" he said with a grin "I will get Osman to drive you. I insist." He took her hand and held it for the longest few seconds. A spark of electricity shot through them both. He raised her hand to his mouth and sensually kissed it like a gentleman. He would have much rather kissed her lush mouth long and hard. He wanted to crush them beneath his own. He was afraid if he did, he would not be able to stop.

She felt her checks flush. Just in the nick of time Osman appeared, otherwise he might have not be able to resist the urge to sweep her off of her feet and take her back up to his room and do unimaginable things to this alluring creature.

She made his whole body want to come back to life. An awakening. He had not been with another woman for three years.

Sleep would not come easy tonight.

Curled up in her own bed which now felt too big on her own, she too was finding it hard to sleep. Her hand still tingled from his tender kiss. All she could do was to think about his lips on hers. What would he taste like? And those oh so sexy eyes. The night was long and endless. Sleep did not come easy for her until nearly dawn.

CHAPTER 6

They entered the Kapalicarsi through one of its many stone archways. The Grand Bazaar was hectic and very noisy. There were stalls with leather goods, colourful scarfs and all sorts of touristy items, some with clothes and other with wooded carvings. Others with brightly painted pottery. The sound of people haggling for best prices rang in her ears. Unusual smells tickled her nose. It was like an indoor city of its own.

"Does everyone shop like this?"

"Most. It is a tradition." Ahmet answered.

"I am not sure I could do this every day. There must be hundreds of shops?"

"I believe there something like 3000 shops and stalls, maybe more."

"How do people know where to go? It's like a Labyrinth in here."

"After a couple of visits, you will get the hang of it."

"I hope so."

As they walk through the crowd Lou-Ann gasp as she saw a window of stunning oriental belly dance costumes covered in shinney jewels. Halise pulled on her Fathers sleeve. He winked at the small child hanging on his arm.

"Come on, let's go in and look."

"I can't afford those."

"Who said anything about buying, were only looking. It is all part of the experience."

They wondered through the door to be greeted by even more exquisite garments and a friendly face. Ahmet spoke to the shop keeper and they smiled.

"Oh My Gosh, they are so beautiful. Oh look, I love this one. Oooohh! I like this one too! There are so many to choose from." Then she stopped dead with her jaw wide opened. "Oh wow! Look at this. This is the one." It was a sumptuous purple gown with gold trim and heavily jewelled studded bra top with gold brocade and a matching scarf. That too was adorned with tiny matching jewels that twinkled like tiny stars on a dark night. She looked at the price tag. Her smiled turned upside down into a frown. It was way out of the price range. She could ever afford such a luxury. The tag read 2.800 lira.

The shop keeper asked her if she would like to try it on, she shook her head. She just knew it would fit like it had been made for her and couldn't bear the disappointment of not purchasing for herself.

The two men and Halise were chatting away in their native tongue and then with a nod of the head they shook hands.

"Maybe next time." She said with a wry smile. "Maybe I will come back before I go home to London." Knowing full well she would have to buy a cheaper version if she did come back let alone find the place again in this amazing maize of walkways and shops.

The shop keeper smiled at her and gave her his business card. This made her chuckle. It said ALI BARBAR'S OREINTAL BELLY DANCE DESIGHNS along with the address and telephone number. She put it in her bag and politely said thank you. They then returned to the hustle and bustle of the main walkways.

On several occasions their arms or hands grazed each other. Accidental or on purpose or even from the crush of the crowd it made them both tingle with delight. It felt good for both of them and each time it happened they became more aware of each other's presence.

They broke free of the crowd when Lou-Ann spotted a colourful vase that she thought Jane would like.

"How much is this vase please. The stall holder plucked a figure out of the air and grinned. He told her it was 80 lira, which was far too rich for her.

Halise and her father stood by her side her. He whispered in her ear. It made her catch her breath as his hot vapours touched her neck.

"Start very low, offer him say, 15. You must haggle."

She would do her best.

"15" She replied

"65" He retorted

"25" She grinned innocently and looked back at her two accomplices. The haggling continued.

"5o liras for the pretty lady and her daughter." That made Halise smile. She thought she would give it one more try.

"40 liras. That's my final offer?" She held out her hand and the seller shook it.

"We have a deal pretty lady. Cheap as chips." He said cheekily.

She let out a sigh of relief as she handed over the cash. He wrapped the vase in newspaper to protect it. She was happy with her first haggling experience.

"That was fun." Lou-Ann said happily.

"I am glad you are having fun today. Shall we eat?"

They went down another alleyway where some food vendors had set up shop. They found a suitable place to sit and eat. They all had the same, a tasty chicken kebab on a Turkish flat bread and can of soft drink to wash it down.

"Lou-Ann, will you teach me to dance?" Halise piped up taking them by surprise.

"What would you like to learn?" Lou-Ann responded

"Well, I think I would like to become a ballerina."

"You will have to ask your father but I don't have a problem with that."

"I think that will be ok. You could move some things around in gym. We will have to get you some shoes and things. I will call Osman he will know where to go. It's probably the only thing you can't buy in here.

"You have a gym! I don't know why that surprises me."

"It's next to the pool and Jacuzzi."

"You have a pool and a Jacuzzi? Lou-Ann said even more surprised.

"I like swimming too." Halise chimed in.

"We can come back here another day. Let's find our way out of here and meet Osman." Ahmet added.

The ever-resourceful Osman new the perfect place to take them. He always knew were to get anything you needed. Ahmet parted with what she thought was an exceptional amount of money but he didn't even bat an eye lid. It made his daughter happy and that was all that mattered. He had also insisted on paying for her things too. Halise had come out with the whole kit and caboodle. Ballet slippers, tap shoes, pink leg warmers and tights. Halise had insisted on even getting a pink tutu and a pink bag to keep it all in. She had looked irresistible in the costume and the sales assistant didn't even have to try too hard. Lou-Ann bent down to Halise's height.

"We will start Monday afternoon as soon as I get to your house Ok, when I finish my rehearsals."

The child screeched in delight and clapped her hands with excitement.

Rehearsals started at 9.30 prompt Monday morning. Lou-Anne had arrived a good 15 minutes early to try to make a good impression. She was not the first to have turn up, though she still had not seen Claudia. Madame Massari kept checking her watch to make sure she started on time. She hated tardiness and would not stand for any nonsense.

Claudia turned up with seconds to spare. Madame Massari gave her a cutting look.

"Sorry Madame Massari, I will be extra early tomorrow." Claudia muffled with her head down. She did not want her teacher knowing she was nursing a hangover. She gave Lou-Ann a gruff hello and a wry smile.

The class started on time even with one girl missing. Eventually she turned up just a few minutes late and Madame Massari gave out to her will both barrels.

"You think this is a holiday. Do you? I will not tolerate tardiness." The girl's excuse of not knowing where the venue was just wasn't going to cut it. Everyone knew from that moment on she was going to be a hard task master. There would be blood, sweat and tears for before time was up.

Claudia, even after a vodka-soaked night, thought she was better than everyone else. It could have just been her demeanour but she seemed to make tutting noise when someone wrong. Lou-Ann even over-heard her what sounded like sarcastic remarks in Russian.

They had a short break at 11.15 to rehydrate and cool off. Everyone was already exhausted and soaked with sweat. The girls were an eclectic mix. There was another Russian girl who was the total opposite to the cocky blonde. Some Egyptian girls that obviously had work with Madame Massari before. They picked up her moves easily and half a dozen Turkish girls. Lou-Ann was the only British girl there. She felt a little alone and inadequate. At the end of their break her calf where still hurting her. She realized how out of shape she was. She thought how much they would hurt tomorrow. 1.30 was too far away.

She was looking forward to seeing Halise and starting her lessons though at that moment in time she doubted she would have the energy. What's more she was hoping she would get a glimpse of Ahmet and those tempting eyes of his that made her very core go weak.

At exactly 1.30 Osman appeared to take her back to the house for her first day as Halise's carer. She wished she had had time to change and Shower but no one was going to see her in her sweat soak clothes. She would sort herself out back at the house.

To her surprise the car door opened apparently by itself. She climbed in to be greeted by Ahmet. His eyes lit up with delight. As usual she blushed.

"You look like you have had a busy morning Miss Masters, sorry Lou-Ann, we were close by and I have a few hours till my next meeting so I thought I would come home for lunch."

"I wish I had known; I would have changed before I got in the car. I am a mess."

"It is ok. It a sign of hard word. Madame Massari is a bit of a task master, isn't she?"

"Absobloodylutley." She forgot whose company she was in for a moment. "Ooops, I'm sorry."

"Not a problem" They both laughed it off.

They pulled outside the house but used the side door that led straight into the kitchen.

"We will lunch in here today if that's ok with you Zita?"

The kitchen was large and cool and Zita was bustling around. The air was filled with the smell of freshly baked flatbreads and scented chicken.

"You have time to freshen up before we eat. You can use the showers in the gym." Ahmet gave her instructions were to go and told her to use the towels provided.

She appeared back ten minutes later refreshed and feeling hungry. Halise was waiting to greet her in her usual over enthusiastic fashion.

"Merhaba." The child greeted her then her mouth turned down "Pappa would not let me change into my ballet things until after lunch in case I spilt anything on them."

"Well I am afraid your father is right and very wise. But soon we will turn you into a Prima ballerina. So, my little angel let's eat our lunch then we can get started. I am Starving." She sat down at the table next to Halise and whispered in the little girl's ear. "Madame Massari is a slave driver." They both giggled. Zita served up a simple but tasty lunch.

When they were all finished and the conversation came to an end, Zita cleared away the table. Lou-Ann offered to help.

"NO, no! You are guest." Zita had insisted that she do it herself.

"Lou-Ann and I will go to the gym and prepare it. Some equipment still needs rearranging. So Halise if you go and get your things from your room you can meet us there in a few minutes." Halise did as she was instructed for a change with no argument. She skipped off happily to her princess bedroom.

Lou-Ann followed Ahmet back to the gym where she had showered. He opened the door for her and invited her to enter. He closed it swiftly behind and stared into her eyes.

Ahmet moved closer to her. She knew her was going to kiss her. What's more she realized she wanted him to kiss her, long and hard.

A no holds bards' kind of kiss. Her pulse raced. She could feel the heat of his breath on her face. It felt like a scorching breeze from a hot desert. His smouldering eyes never leaving hers, it was like her was searching her soul. She felt the pit of her stomach tighten. She knew should back away but her feet wouldn't move. He came even closer towards her and brushed his lips against hers. She knew she should stop, he was forbidden fruit, her employer. He intensified the kiss and his tongue parted her willing lips. His arms slipped around her waist pulling her as close as he could get. She gave back what he was giving her, pure pleasure. Her forbidden fruit tasted delicious. The voice in her head said stop but her heart cried out for more.

A happy child's voice could be heard in the hallway singing her heart out. It was Halise. He pulled away quickly, leaving her flushed and desperately wanting more. Her head spinning and feeling a little confused. No man had ever kissed with such passion, not even Zak. Her whole body was on fire. He turned on his heels and head to the door. With his hand on the door handle Ahmet turned and smiled a devilish grin and left just in the nick of time. It was all should could do to stay standing. She just had seconds to recover before Halise walked in. Her heart still racing and still feeling a little flushed.

"Dam those sexy eyes" She muttered under breath.

"Are you ok?" Halise asked clutching her little pink bag.

"Yes, I am fine. Let's get you changed."

"I think my Pappa likes you."

"Oh do you now. What makes you say that?"

"Well," Halise started "He smiles all the time now. When you are here in the house, Pappa smiles even more."

"Ok little madam, enough of that." She had a sudden guilty pang. "Come on let's start your lessens. Ballet first. Yes!"

"Oh yes please." The little one answered with a huge smile of her own. With that she helped change her put on her leotard and new ballet pumps. Lou-Ann found it hard to concentrate but made it through the lesson with Halise. She was smart for one so young.

They were playing outside in the garden in the shade of the gazebo with a few dolls from Halise's room. It was about 4.30 when Zita came and found them.

"Mr Bahar he send note. Taxi is waiting. Halise stay here."

Puzzled she opened the note

Be ready to go out at 6. Dress smart but comfortable. Ahmet. XX

She said her good-byes to Halise and promised they would continue their game tomorrow. Her heart began to race again.

CHAPTER 7

When Lou-Ann reached the hotel, her heart was still skipping beats with anticipation. She almost skipped to her room like a love-sick teenager. She held the note close to her chest. There was just enough time to do what she needed to do before being picked up again.

She ran the shower in the en suite, the water was refreshing as it ran over her body. She stood under the shower daydreaming for far too long. Her nipples hardened as she thought of him. She wrapped herself in the fluffy towels and headed the wardrobe. Her clothes were quite simple; she hadn't really packed anything suitable for a date. A date, is that was what this was. Oh my! She thought. She pulled out a long white linen skirt and short sleeve wrap over shirt in sky blue and a pair of silver thong sandals. There was no time to do anything fancy with her hair so simple style would have to suffice.

A quick rough dry and a twist and barrette clip would do the job. She left some curls out to soften her face and left it to topple over the clip. It would have been a waste of time to try and straighten her wayward hair, it would only curl and frizz with humidity. Besides time was not on her side.

Not one for too much make up she riffled through her makeup bag and added the finish touches with some pale pink lip gloss and mascara. Ready. The butterflies were creeping back as she wondered what he wanted.

Ready with a few minutes to spare Lou-Ann looked at herself in the mirror

"Not bad, not bad at all." Her reflection smiled back in agreement. Picking up a little silver clutch bag she wondered down to the lobby.

Osman appeared shortly after her own arrival.

"Miss Masters, Mr Bahar sends his apologies." Her heart sank, for a moment she thought Ahmet had decided to cancel. "He has some business to take care of in town. He will meet you there, the car is outside. I shall drive you to meet him."

"Thank you, Osman." A sigh of relief washed over her.

Osman performed his usual ritual of opening the door for her. The car was cool with its air con on max. The drive didn't take long considering the time of day. He pulled over near a main tram stop at the top of a main shopping street and parked at the end of a taxi rank. This time Osman didn't get out of the car. When the door did open a familiar hand was offered to her. She accepted and slipped out of the car gracefully. She blushed a little when she looked up to face remembering his kiss.

"Hungry?" Ahmet enquired.

"A little."

"Let's go eat then, I know just the place." It was hard to think just about food with her by his side. Ahmet tried hard to think of other things but he just wanted to kiss her again and feel his body against hers. They walked for a while in silence until Lou-Ann decided to talk about his daughter to break the ice.

"Halise is very bright little girl for her age," She wondered where they were heading as an old rickety tram passed them and tooted. "she picks things up easily. You must be very proud?"

"I am. She has become my whole life. She is what I work so hard for. I know I spoil her but I can't help it."

As they walked a little further down the hill another of the old-fashioned trams passed them on it was back up to the top. They soon came to a small opening with a stained glass arched window. If you didn't know it was there you would walk right by. As they entered, she noticed there were several restaurants all touting for business in a glass covered alley way. There was a short round jolly man in a waste coat in a crisp white apron who held out his hand to greet Ahmet. It was obvious they knew each other.

"Merhaba Mr Bahar, my old friend. Merhaba. Hosgeldiniz. Welcome Miss." They exchanged a hearty greeting. "It's been a long time Mr Bahar, Miss, please follow me." He led them to a cosy spot at the first restaurant on the right-hand side. "Would this be ok for you or you want to eat inside?"

Ahmet looked to Lou-Ann for an answer.

"Here would be lovely thank you."

The waiter pulled out a chair for her and nodded at Ahmet.

There were several other couples and families seated at various restaurants and a medley of aromas emanating from all around tantalized her taste buds.

The waiter came back with a basket of breads and some lemon iced water and proceeded to fill their water glasses, another followed with plate of appetizers and laid them on the table. They looked delicious especially the feta cheese and beetroot salad. There was a small portion calamari and some humus. The waiter grinned

"Teşekkür ederim"

"Wine Mr Bahar?" the waiter handed him a wine menu.

"Red Ok for you Lou-Ann?" She agreed with a smile. "We will have a bottle of no 29 please."

"Excellant choice Mr Bahar!"

The waiter strode of with a grin on his face as I he knew something they didn't.

Once they were on their own again, he grazed his fingers across the tops of hers. Their eyes met.

"I am sorry about earlier, I crossed the line and I shouldn't have kissed you like that earlier." Lou-Ann went to interrupt

"Ahmet please."

"No, let me finish. I must confess I have wanted to kiss you since the moment I laid eyes on you. When I saw you at lunch time for some reason, I found you totally irresistible. I barely managed the journey home. But once again I am sorry."

Lou-Ann was a bit taken aback at Ahmet's confession but she had one of her own.

"Ahmet," She took his hand a little firmer and tried to string some words together to explain her own feelings. "Please don't apologise, I am glad you did, though I was a little shocked."

They both breathed a sigh of relief.

"Well that is somewhat of a relief." He disclosed. "And by the way you look beautiful this evening and I have a desperate urge to kiss you again." Lou-Ann and Ahmet both chuckled like a pair of school children.

"If you are a good boy, I might just let you." She said coyly.

After that the rest of the evening was more relaxed and comfortable. The food was amazing and the conversation flowed easily. To anyone else they looked like star-crossed lovers that had been together for ever. Ahmet paid the bill and shook his old friend's hand firmly and spoke briefly. The waiter had obviously been glad to see his old customer return especially with the large tip Ahmet had left. He promised not to leave it so long till his next visit. They left through the spectacular ornate glass arch which now was lit up with lights from the restaurants making the reds and greens glow.

They started to walk back up the hill.

"We will have to get a taxi as I have given Osman the rest of the night off. I thought he and Zita deserve some time together." He raised a suggestive eyebrow. "I shall take you to your Hotel if that is agreeable.

"That would be fine. You are such a gentleman Mr Bahar."

"That's what I want you to think." He winked "I understand you had a gruelling morning with Madam Massari?"

"Just a little. Everyone else is so good." He held out his hand for her to take. She took it gladly and smiled as they walked the to the Taxi rank. A warm fuzzy feeling ran through her.

Ahmet felt like a dark cloud had been lifted from his shoulders. He could feel threads of happiness run through his veins. Time to look forward and move on. He would never forget his wife but she would want him to have a normal life. Maybe Lou-Ann was the answer.

They reached the large plaza were life was still bustling along. Trams going this way and that and Taxis touting for business. They hailed a bright yellow taxi with its fair share of dents on it, not something Ahmet was used to doing. They slid in and he put his arm around her shoulders. They turned to look at each other and he kissed her lips softly.

Just before they arrived at the hotel Ahmet looked at Lou-Ann with a wry smile.

"You may think I am being forward but I have an idea." He paused with anticipation. "Why don't you move into the annex at my home, it would make life a lot simpler for everyone. What's more would Halise would be delighted.

"Oh. Um." She replied in shock.

"I am sorry. At least think about it." He was a little embarrassed.

"Ok I will."

"You will think about it?"

She shook her head.

"NOPE! I won't think about it." Ahmet looked a little confused. "I totally agree with you. If am going to be at your house most of the time it only makes sense, just for convenience you understand. Don't tell Halise. Let's surprise her."

"So tomorrow then?"

"No tomorrow is not ok." She replied. Ahmet looked even more confused. "Waite for me in the taxi, I will be 10 minutes." His expression turned to one of surprise. "Why put off till tomorrow what you can do today." With that she jumped out of the car and left Ahmet sitting speechless in the yellow taxi.

This young vivacious girl just stole his heart. Right there, right then.

As promised, she was back in a flash carrying with her all her worldly goods. She hadn't even bothered to wait for the Skinny bell hop to help her.

Lou-Ann settled quickly into the room in the annex. Halise jumped for joy at breakfast when she saw Lou-Ann. The next few days were pretty much the same, tears and tantrums at rehearsals and then back to new temporary residence to take care of Halise for the afternoon so Zita could get on with her chores. In the evening they sat around the table and ate dinner like a family. Halise would then insist that Lou-Ann take her to bed and tuck her in with a bedtime story. Afterwards she would take apple tea with Ahmet in the gazebo in the garden before she retired to her quarters.

He had not tried to kiss her since Monday and now it was Friday. She wondered if he had changed his mind about her. Secretly she hoped he hadn't. She wanted to feel his lips against once more.

Tonight, she had decided to retire early after their tea drinking ritual and couldn't bare another evening without at least a kiss.

The sun was just lowering itself into bed keeping the evening air warm as they took tea on the patio. The sky turned a shade of burnt orange with tinges of purple. She stood up to face the fabulous sunset.

"WOW!" Lou-Ann gasped. "The sky is so beautiful this evening." She heard the patio chair move then felt his hand on her shoulder and his breath on her neck. Her heart raced. He moved the hair way from her neck and kissed her nape whilst slipping his arms around her waist. He could no longer resist her.

"Not as beautiful as you my askim." As he kissed her for a second time, she could feel her knees quiver. Lou-Ann could barely turn to face him for trembling. As she did their lips brushed then he kissed her slowly and sensually. She could do nothing else but respond.

As their lips parted, Ahmet blurted out.

"Stay right there." He pulled away from her and walked back into the house. It felt like he had been gone for ever, but in reality, it was barley a few minutes.

He returned wearing an enormous smile hardly containing his own excitement. In his arms he held out a cream oblong box tied with a purple ribbon laced with gold. The same colours as the oriental outfit they had seen at the Grand Bazar.

The penny dropped "Oh Ahmet you didn't?"

"Open it and see." She took the box and placed it on the table. With hands shacking with excitement she placed her fingertips on each corner of the purple and pulled it slowly undone. Lou-Ann held her breath as she lifted the lid whilst Ahmet didn't take his eyes of her beaming face. Lining the box was gold tissue paper keeping the contents secret for a little longer. The tissue paper rustled and whispered "open me" as she touched it to reveal the secret inside. She lifted the final layer to reveal the stunning outfit from Ali Barbar's. She had trouble finding the words.

"Oh my word. Oh Ahmet! You shouldn't have."

"I wanted to do something nice for you. You have been so kind to Halise. It is the least I can do."

"It is far too extravagant." She chocked as her eyes pooled with tears of happiness at the over generous gift. She through her arms around his neck in appreciation, then proceeded to take it out of the box then pulled up the top and held it against herself. He raised his eyebrow in amusement. Ahmet new she would look as sexy as hell in it. He tried to ignore the sudden rush of blood to his cock.

"Well it is yours."

"I guess I have no option but to except. Thank you so much. I love it." Lou-Ann kissed him quickly on his cheek in gratitude.

"Tomorrow we will go and do something nice together with Halise. Maybe we can visit the Blue Mosque or one of the old royal palaces?" He said trying to take his mind of what his groin was thinking.

"That would be wonderful. I shall dig out my guidebook that Jane bought me."

"Great. We will have lunch out as well. That's settled!"

CHAPTER 8

Jane heard the letter box rattle as she was just finishing getting ready for work on the Friday morning. I amongst the bills and circulars was Lou-Ann's post card. With delight she read the words scribbled on the back.

Hotel is Amazing {see picture in front}. Room is amazing. Settled in ok. The heat is ridiculous. Burnt my nose just as you I would. Lol. Can't wait to get started. Love you lots. You're the best bestie. Lou-Ann xxx

Jane placed the post card on the tall plant pot stand in her hallway with a lanky Buzzy Lizzie trailing down its sides. She would read it again when she got home. The post card had made her chuckle. She knew what Lou-Ann's fair skin was like. *Typical* Jane thought. The arrival of her friend's post card had set her up for the day though she would still worry that she had done the right thing.

With that she popped on her sandals and picked her bag up and set off for work.

CHAPTER 9

The trip to the Sultans Palace was a resounding success apart from the heat of the afternoon. It stood high on the hill standing proud of its premium position in the city, standing guard to the entrance of the Golden Horn. But safely nestled behind the old city walls.

Lou-Ann found the treasury particularly intriguing. The anti-chambers were full of exquisite priceless relics and jewellery of which Ahmet could appreciate the skills, time and dedication it would have taken the craftsmen to make such stunning artefacts. He even pointed out the ruby and diamond handled dagger that legend had it was made by his ancestors. There were tiny broaches delicately encrusted with all sorts of precious jewels and hair combs with diamonds and pearls.

Ahmet explained how they would have been made and said most of the techniques would have remained the same over the centuries.

The other rooms were filled with sumptuous ancient embroidered silk costumes from the Imperial wardrobe and clothing made with the finest lace with silver and gold threads. Other rooms had ancient pottery from China that was said to have change colour if it was too come into contact with poison. Other dinning sets set were set in giant cabinets alongside stunning crystal ware and huge silver platters. In the armoury there were long pike poles and swords of all shapes and sizes. All would have been used in battle at some point. The Topkapi Palace was a full of many wondrous things.

"In its heyday it must have been like its own city with people hustling and bustling all over the place." Lou-Ann chimed.

The other side of the courtyard was the Harem, the lavish quarters for the Sultans wives, his many children and concubines. Lou-Ann mused over the idea of one man having so many women to tend to. How would have the Sultan found the time and strength to service them all and run Constantinople at the same time. She smiled to herself.

"Well he must have been a very busy man." Lou-Ann said

"Very!" Ahmet replied through a smile.

Throughout the day a discreet tension was growing between them. The smiles and gazes they gave each made them both tingle with desire.

Halise was holding on to Lou-Ann's hand. Eventually Ahmet put his arm around Lou-Ann's waist. The little girl beamed from ear to ear to see her Pappa happy. Happy with Lou-Ann. The apparent family enjoyed the rest of the afternoon walking round the well-kept walled gardens eating ice cream with the light scent of sweet summer flowers floating on the occasional breeze.

Eventually Halise's little legs gave out and her Pappa scooped up a tired but very happy girl and carried her. A phone call and a short time later Osman swiftly appeared outside the gates to whisk them away on a red magic flying carpet.

Osman announced that Zita was already preparing a light evening meal for them to enjoy on their return.

Halise had plenty to chat about over dinner, relaying the whole day to Zita and Osman.

Sometimes in English and other times Turkish. One comment Hallies made Turkish in particular made Ahmet blush and Zita grin.

Everyone was happy.

Lou-Ann was amazed how quickly Halise switched between the two languages. She made a promise to learn some Turkish words before her trip was over. She would get Halise to help her with some basics.

CHAPTER 10

Jane had stayed in by herself for the second Friday in a row. She was missing her best friend's company. She had picked up a no 138A from the Chinese take away. A meal for one would have to make do washed down with an ice-cold Budweiser and the television would have to keep her company.

A constant ringing of the doorbell and a huge bang on the flat door and disturbed her. A rather slurred familiar voice was ranting behind it. She was surprised to see Zak through the window.

"Where's my Annie, I want to speak to her. Let me in." Zak banged the door even harder." Let me in Jane, I want to speak to my wife." He demanded with his finger on the bell constantly. Though it wasn't that late she didn't want the neighbours disturbed. With reservation she opened the door a jar.

"She's not here Zak." Peering round the door "Go home and sleep it off."

"Where's is she Jane? Where's my wife?" He slurred. Jane opened the door properly. She could smell the alcohol on his breath.

"Come inside Zak." He swayed into the hallway. Jane closed the door behind him." She has gone away for a few weeks. I told you she wasn't here."

"I may be a little worse for wear but I know you know where she is." At that moment he spied the post card in the hall leaning against the Buzzy Lizzie plant pot. "I'm sorry Jane maybe I shouldn't have come here." He bumbled a little further in to the flat. "I went to her flat and it's up for sale. I assumed she'd moved back in with you again." He almost sounded genuinely disappointed.

"Take a seat in the front room Zak. I'll put the kettle on then I'll call you a cab." As she turned her back, he palmed the post card and tried to read it before Jane returned. He had guessed right; it was from his estranged wife.

"Still take your coffee black Zak?" Jane shouted from her tiny kitchen.

"Yes please." He slurred. "One sugar." Zak fumbled around in his arm jacket pocket to find his mobile phone. Trying to hold his hand steady he took 2 pictures, one of the front and one of the back. Zak's alcohol-soaked mind raced. The card not only had the picture of the hotel on the front it had the address on the back. He was sure he could find it and then find his Lou-Ann. He put the post card in his pocket intending to put it back on his way out.

Half way through his coffee the cab beeped outside. Zak apologised again and went home to sleep it off. Or so Jane thought!

"Bloody men!" Jane muttered as she locked up. She wouldn't tell Lou-Anne that he had been there. It would only upset her. She eventually went off to bed and didn't notice the card wasn't were she left it.

CHAPTER 11

Walking down the stairs from her new nightly ritual of a bedtime story and tucking Halise safely in her bed, Lou-Ann heard Ahmet's voice coming from the white marble waiting room where she was ushered into on her first visit to the house. She couldn't understand what he was saying but she assumed he was taking a business call on his phone.

When Lou-Ann reached the doorway, she saw Ahmet sitting on the cushioned covered two-seater. He was holding his head in his hands looking like he had the weight of the world on his shoulders.

"I thought I heard you talking to someone?"

"I am, I was." He sighed with a heavy heart. "I was talking to Malia." She moved in front of him and took his hand in hers. He lifted his head and she looked deep into those dark mysterious eyes of his quizzically.

"I was telling her about you."

"And what did you tell her?"

"I told her that you were beautiful and that you have a special bond with Halise," He half smiled "and that when I am around you, I feel alive again. That you make my heart dance. You make me smile all the time even when I am not with you. I think about you all the time." He moved the hair from her face. "I haven't felt like this for a long time my askim. You make me want to come home at the end of the day."

"Oh Ahmet!" She was choked.

"I also asked her for forgiveness. I feel Guilty for the way you make me feel, guilty for falling in love with you." A weight lifted as his admission fell off his lips.

"You have fallen in love with me?"

"Evet, Miss Lou-Ann Masters, yoy seviyorum." He kissed her gently on her check. "But I also need her forgiveness for what I am about to do."

She felt his arm slip round her back, he pulled her close and crushed her sweet lips hard and wantonly against his own. A pang of guilt niggled her inside. Now was not the time to reveal her own secret.

She pulled slightly away from his hard body.

"Maybe you should ask for her blessing instead. Melia would want you to be happy." With that he scooped her up into his arms and kissed her hungrily again. She couldn't help herself and let her tongue weave in and out with his. He carried her up the stairs to his room. The love making was like a natural phenomenon of volcanic proportions.

After their worlds had collided, they slept contently. They slept entwined in each other's arms like two lost pieces of a jigsaw puzzle that had been reunited. A perfect match.

As daylight broke Lou-Ann woke up in the exact same place where she had fallen asleep, cradled in Ahmet's loving arms. Cradled in the man's arms she loved. Really loved. The realization of how she felt had hit her like a bolt from the blue. Ahmet Bahar had stolen her broken heart and fixed it. She lay a soft kiss on her lovers check so not to wake him.

"I love you Mr Bahar." She whispered before she slid out from the tangled cotton sheets. She thought it best to go back to the annex in case Halise came into her father's room as she often did in the mornings.

Picking up her scattered clothes from around the bedroom floor she headed for the door when she heard the sheets rustle and her name her name being spoken softly.

"Lou-Ann don't leave, stay with me. Come back to bed." He looked at her longingly in the shadows of the dawn, "Bring that beautiful body back to me."

Still clutching her clothes "What about Halise, she might wake up early and come in."

"This is true. Lock the door then we won't have to worry." His lips curled "I have something that needs your urgent attention." She locked the door, dropped her clothes back in heap on the floor, and then seductively sauntered over slowly to the bed. She stood there naked in all her glory. His cock flexed and grew harder.

"Why Mr Bahar, I have absolutely no idea what you are talking about." She replied innocently as she slinked around to his side of the bed. The sheets were all at sixes and sevens from the night before. As she straddled his hard, masculine body, she could feel his erection growing between their bodies.

"I love you too Askim."

He had heard her confession.

Her body slid slowly over his manhood. She was already aroused with the thought of him inside her. Throwing her head back she rode him hard and fast whilst he bucked beneath her like a wild stallion. His breath grew rapid as he clutched one hand on her cute behind, the other teasing her pert breast. Those oily eyes never lift her face. He watched her rise and fall in perfect rhythm. They shared a thunderous orgasm like nothing before.

Breathless, they collapsed into each other's arms. They fell back to sleep, sated and satisfied.

The bond of love had been sealed.

CHAPTER 12

Zak's drunken plan had come to fruition with him landing at Ataturk airport. It hadn't even occurred to him she might not want him back. His ego was riding high. He was Zak Hopkins, everyone wanted to jump his bones.

Zak grabbed his holdall from the overhead locker, disembarked, paid his visitors tax and headed out of the airport. He flagged a yellow cab and jumped in.

He showed the driver the post card, agreed a price then set off to the city. The journey was hot and sweaty. The traffic was heavy. A completely different experience to the journey Lou-Ann had made in the air-conditioned beamer.

The taxi eventually pulled up outside the white building that replicated the photo on the picture post card. Zak paid the driver thankful he had arrived in one piece, exited the cab and headed for the entrance of the hotel.

The door man was dressed in a traditional white out fit with curly toed shoes with pompoms on. He opened the door for Zak. He nodded in appreciation. The same pretty receptionist was sitting there with her unusually beautiful smile waiting greet the guests.

"Merhaba Sir. Karsilama. Can I help you?" She had spotted the British flag stitched on his holdall and just assumed he was English. He turned on the Zak charm and gave her a sly wink.

"Well Merhaba to you, you beautiful creature. I think maybe you can." Being the smarmy, flirtatious, bastard he was. "I am looking for someone who is staying here, Mrs Lou-Ann Hopkins."

She looked at the register and shook her head.

"I am very sorry Sir, there is no one with that name staying here, and you are?"

"I am her, Um, brother, Zak Hopkins, you must have. She sent me this post card." He pulled out the post card from his pocket. "Please check the computer again for me babe, Mrs LOU-ANN HOPKINS." As if saying it slower and louder would help. She tapped away at the console for a second or two then smiled at him.

"NO. No body of that name is registered. We did have a Miss Lou-Ann Masters but she is no longer a resident here."

"Small, pretty dark-haired girl?"

"Yes Sir."

"Do you know where she went?" Zak enquired.

"Your timing is perfect Mr Hopkins your sister is here having afternoon tea with the owner's brother. I will ring through and let them know you are here."

"Thank you," he paused and read her name tag "Deani. Maybe we can hook up and have lunch sometime." Zak winked at her again. He grabbed his bag and started walking to the restaurant.

"Sir, Sir. Mr Hopkins," She shouted out after him. "You cannot…" But before she could finish her sentence and reach for the phone had had gone. She dialled the extension as quick as she could to warm Mr Bahar that someone was looking for his lunch companion.

Ahmet and Lou-Ann were sitting opposite each other holding a long cold glass of champagne in one hand and Ahmet laid his spare hand over hers and gently stroked her fingers. They had enjoyed a romantic morning together as well as their bodies. The Champagne was just their way of celebrating the happiness they had discovered in each other's arms the previous night.

They had heard the telephone ringing in the background but by time the call was answered it was too late.

Zak entered the dining room as bold as brass.

"Well, well, well. You two look really cosy together." He grinned. "Gone back to your maiden name have you Mrs Hopkins?" His tone was dry.

Ahmet released her hand as Lou-Ann blinked in disbelief. She couldn't quite grasp who or what she was seeing.

"What the bloody hell are you doing here?" She responded in horror.

"I've come to take my little wife home. You know, try to make another go if it." Zak held his hand out to offer a handshake to the gentleman sitting opposite *his* wife. Ahmet declined. "Zak Hopkins and you are?" It was obvious Ahmet had no idea about Lou-Ann's predicament when his jaw hit the floor and an invisible Knife stabbed at his heart.

"Oh dear!" The words were sarcastic. "Let me guess, she didn't tell you she was married, did she?"

Ahmet just sat there in utter disbelief hardly comprehending the words that fell out of the stranger's mouth. Wanting and waiting for some kind of explanation. Wanting and waiting for her deny the revelation.

"Ahmet!" she cried, "I am so sorry, I can explain." She glanced away from Ahmet and stared and Zak. She wanted to knock that malicious grin of his face but words would have to be enough. "How the bloody hell did you find me and what's more what right do you have to come bursting back into my life? You can't expect me to follow you home like a little lost dog." She ranted on. "It's over Zak. You're wondering dick made sure of that." It was everything she had wanted to say but never had the chance or the balls. Lou-Ann fort back her angry tears.

"That was easy, Jane's postcard babe." He flashed the post card at her still grinning, thinking how clever he was. "Aren't you going to introduce me to your friend my love?"

"No. I am not and I'm not sure why I should. What's more I am defiantly *NOT* your love or your babe. Not since you slept with that tart." She seethed desperately trying to maintain her decorum.

Ahmet stood up trying to stay level-headed.

"Please sit down, you are causing a scene." He pointed to a chair and tried to be polite in front of the other customers. Luckily there wasn't many.

"No thanks. WE won't be long. Let's go little wifey. I haven't come all this way to go home on my own." His voice turned sinister.

"We." She huffed. "We are not going anywhere together. Not now, not ever." Tears started to leak from the corners of her eyes as her cheeks reddened with fury.

Zak lowered his voice and changed tactics. Time to turn up the charm. Meanwhile Ahmet was getting angrier and more uncomfortable by the intrusion but tried to keep calm and not add to the situation. The realisation that his new love was married was sinking in even though he appeared to be total idiot. There had to be a reason why she had not told him of her marriage. What's more Ahmet was not going to let Zak see his distain and disappointment. He was in love with her. He felt it in his heart and he was sure there wasn't anything that they couldn't overcome.

He had just found her and was not about to let this stranger take her away.

"Look Annie, I was stupid and I am very sorry. What can I say, I want you back?" He grinned a schoolboy grin that used to make her week at the knees once upon a time.

"You have a nerve Zak." She tried not to raise her voice. "I don't believe you for one second. You a compulsive liar and a cheating womaniser. We are *DONE* Zak Hopkins. I am not going home with you. *EVER*! We are through. *GET IT*? I want you crawl back into whatever cesspit you crawled out of and leave me, us alone. Oh, and by the way I know about your inheritance, your sister told me. Oh, and while you are at it, I want a divorce!" She couldn't believe she let those words finally escape her mouth. It had been a long time coming. By now she was shaking all over.

Ahmet stood to leave to find his brother for support. He could see Lou-Ann was physically distressed by Zak and thought he might need some back up from Akin.

Zak's mood changed again. A look of annoyance crossed his face as he grabbed her wrist as he tried to pull her to her feet.

Ahmet saw red. How dare he touch her so viscously?

"Take your hands of her." He raised his voice and then swore at him in Turkish. "Got deliği."

"Ok, Ok." With that Zak released Lou-Ann's wrist and then took a swing at Ahmet.

"Zak, stop it." She yelled. Thankfully Ahmet moved swiftly out of the way. Zak missed, lost his balance and landed in a heap on the floor.

Akin arrived after hearing the kafuffle and Lou-Ann pleading cries.

"I think it is time for you to leave Sir." Akin ordered with a look of approval from his brother. "Unless you want to find out what it is like to spend the night in a cell at a Turkish police station."

Zak scrambled embarrassingly up off the floor and snatched up his bag and headed to the door. He thought he would leave her with one last parting shot.

"We're not finished yet, not by a long chalk, *BITCH.*" He shouted menacingly.

Ahmet pulled a crying and shaking Lou-Ann to his chest and held her tight and tried to comfort her. He was also shaken up but tried to put a brave face on for her sake. His anger at her had already subsided. He realized Zak was a waste of fresh air. Ahmet loved her and was determined not to let it come between them.

"Let's go home," He took his phone from his pocket and called Osman. "we will talk later." Akin held out his hand to his little brother. They shook a hearty farewell and told him not to worry about the incident.

"I'm so sorry Ahmet, so sorry." Were the only words she could muster. Tears were flowing freely now down her flushed cheeks. Ahmet softy took her hand and led her out to the foyer were the shiny red car was waiting outside.

Akin was set to go Kusadasi on the Monday to join his wife and children and the rest of the family on their summer vacation. What a way to meet his brother's new girlfriend. Fortunately, no real harm was done. He offered the half a dozen customers a free drink on him to smooth things over which were gratefully accepted. Most enjoyed the afternoon's unexpected entertainment.

Zak was creeping sheepishly around the next doorway licking his wounded pride whilst trying to regain his composure. He saw Ahmet and Lou-Ann leave the hotel and climb into the car. He hailed a cab.

"Follow that car, that bastard has my wife." He grunted at the unshaven driver. "If you don't lose them, I'll pay you double." The driver asked no questions and the chance of some extra cash was enough to stick his beat-up old cab into gear, he revved up and followed the beamer.

The cab driver was literally going to take Zak for a ride. By hook or by crook extra cash was always welcome.

The cab hung back and followed the car containing Zak's wife. They weaved through the traffic and finally reached the suburbs.

"Hang back, hang back. Pull over here. Don't want them to spot us do we." Zak ordered as the red BMW pulled up the private driveway.

"Hey Mister. I know this house. I bring lady here a few days ago from her work. Pretty lady. You lucky man."

"You know where she works?" The cab driver nodded. "You could be useful." Zak opened the car door then stuck his head back in the cab. "Wait here for me." He straightened up and gingerly crossed the tree lined road. He made sure no one was watching and that the Bahar car had disappeared from sight before wondering up the private road which lead to the house. He wasn't quite sure what his next move was going to be but he would come up with something.

He became agitated as his blood boiled as it ran through his veins. The thought of her living the high life without him angered him, and as for the whore sleeping with another man made him feel sick to his stomach. She belongs to me, my property, mine! He thought as beads of sweat trickled down his back. He reached the iron gates and made a mental note of the security camera on the wall holding the elaborate metal gates in place. The trees were thick and would make a good hiding place. Noted. The place looked like it wouldn't be easy to gain entrance but as his father would say where there is a will there's a way. Zak headed back to the cab.

"Let's head back into the city. I need a hotel mate. On the way back could you show me were you picked up my wife from last week?"

"Yes sir. I know good cheap place. I ring my cousin and see if there's rooms." That cabby got his phone from his top pocket and rang his cousin whilst turning the car around. "Ok, no problem. 83 euros this ok. It's clean and friendly. You will like I am sure." Before long they were back in the city. The hotel was just as described. What's more it wasn't far from where the driver had picked up Lou-Anne.

He paid his driver the over inflated fair but didn't really care. In turn the driver gave him his businesses card with his mobile number on it. They exchanged glances and Zak understood that this would be the man to call when he needed anything. His go to guy for a price. He settled into his room then found a bar and had a few pints of cooling lager before returning to retire for the day.

Zak had thought his estranged wife would coming running back into his arms once he had apologized especially as he had travelled so far to do it. He hadn't bargained on little mousy Lou-Ann growing a backbone or on her meeting someone else. Especially meeting some rich Turk. He was miffed at the thought that she didn't want him back in her life. *Now she wants a divorce. Bollocks.* Zak thought. Now she will get half of everything including his inheritance from his grandfather which he became entitled upon his marriage to Lou-Ann provided they stay married for a year. It was sort of an insurance, a proviso the doddering old fool had put in his will. This was a little secret was one he forgot to tell his bride.

He had to convince her he was telling the truth. Secretly he just wanted to keep the money for himself and save face with the family. No one got divorced in the Hopkins family. No one!

"She's coming home with me and that's that, despite what she wants." He gruffled to himself. "How dare she humiliate me like that? Bitch. If I can't have her no one can have her. As for that smarmy Turk, he'll get his just desserts you wait and see."

He would have to bide his time and come up with a new plan before striking like a coiled viper.

Zak was determined not to go empty handed. He would watch, wait and listen until the right opportunity presented his self. Despite his Grandfathers draconian ideals, he would get his money. £100.000 wasn't to be sniffed at. He and his 'Wife' would be at the solicitors on the appointed day.

It was no longer about love; it was about money and possession. Not that Love had ever come into it in the first place.

Lou-Ann sat shaking in the back of the car. Ahmet sat next to her still confused about the revelations that had occurred at his brother's hotel just a few moments before. He did his best to calm and comfort her.

"Please, it is ok. Do not cry askim." He placed his arm around her. "This does not change how I feel about you."

"Oh Ahmet, I'm so sorry I didn't say anything. It wasn't as if I knew I was going to fall for you." She sobbed pathetically." I've made a real mess of everything haven't I?"

The journey was a silent one, neither not quite what to say.

When they got home, Zita bought them apple tea. Lou-Ann shook her head in refusal.

"Yes drink, you feel better." Zita held out the small glass to her shaking hands. "Halise gone to play with grandson. 0k Mr Bahar? She explained in broken English. Ahmet thanked Zita as she disappeared.

It seemed that Turkish tea was much the same as British tea, suitable for all occasions and used cure all ills.

Ahmet went to the liquor cabinet and poured her a stiff drink.

"Here, have a brandy instead." Ahmet insisted "It will calm your nerves." She held out her shacking hands still holding her tea. Ahmet replaced one glass for the other. She took a large gulp and grimaced. "Now tell me what has happened, what did that idiot do to you anyway?"

Lou-Ann sniffled and started to try to tell Ahmet about her short marriage and how Zak had cheated on her with just about anything in a skirt. She also now realized he had married her to get his hands on his inheritance.

"He must have thought I was a soft touch. He broke my heart and ruined my life. I couldn't forgive him." Ahmet sat a listened, he felt her pain and anguish and didn't like seeing her this way. "When I auditioned for you I never thought you would even consider me but I had nothing to lose. My passport was still in my maiden name. I just thought it would easier that way."

"From what you tell me that prick didn't deserve you any way."

"I am scared Ahmet, I know him, he won't give up easily".

"Do not worry. You are safe here, I promise. Why don't you go lie down for a while?" As she stood, she felt her legs weaken. Ahmet caught her arm. "Let me help you." He put his arms around her and put her glass on the coffee table then escorted her to her apartment. She thanked him softly for opening her door and guided her to her bedroom. As she sat at the edge Ahmet brushed the hair from her face. "You are so beautiful my askim, how could that idiot treat you that way." He kissed her forehead. She lifted her head and looked into his eyes. She found forgiveness in them. His mouth covered hers. That was enough to let her guard down and started a delightful chain of events.

They lay together for the longest time after he had made sweet slow love to her. Both wishing they didn't ever have to leave each other's embrace.

CHAPTER 13

Monday morning came around all too fast. Lou-Ann could hardly believe what an emotional roller coaster the last few days had been. She had to pinch herself back to reality.

Lou-Ann just about made rehearsals with seconds to spare. She found it hard to concentrate. Her mind was wondering all over the place.

"Miss Masters." Madam Massari shouted when she missed several steps. "What is wrong with you today? Wake up. Pay attention."

"I'm sorry Madam Massari." All she could think about was Ahmet. His kiss. His touch and those dam, sexy come to bed eyes and, oh my god, those sensual hands running all over her body. Now was most definitely not the appropriate time to come over all unnecessary. The whole cast was looking at her.

Three and a half hours of gruelling rehearsals in 38-degree heat was more than most could bear. The air conditioning seemed to be virtually nonexistent and made no difference to the still hot air. Even water didn't quench her thirst. Everyone was sweat stained and exhausted.

It wasn't particularly hotter than any other day but the air felt thinner and heavier.

"OK, listen everyone." Madam Massari clapped her hands loudly. "Once more time from the beginning. Let's set it right this time please." Even she sounded like she had had enough of the exhausting heat.

"Slave driver." Lou-Ann muttered under her breath not thinking anyone else would here.

"You have something to say Miss Masters?" She felt like a naughty schoolgirl just about to be sent to detention.

"No Madame Massari." She averted her eyes to the floor, embarrassed.

"Ok, if it's ok with you Miss Masters we will carry on, maybe we go home a little early today if it is correct."

The thought of a leaving a few moments early seemed to buck everyone up a little. With a renewed vigour as they started to dance to the music started again.

They were rehearsing for the finally. Diva Claudia was placed centre stage where she shimmied her skinny Russian backside. But then what did she expect. She was an exceptional dancer and she knew it.

After they had finished, as promised they were released for the day. Claudia approached Lou-Ann.

"Come. You have drink with us? You have time. Yes? We finish early, yes?"

"I don't think so, thanks for asking any way." She responded to Claudia's sudden interest in her.

"Yes, yes you come, it will be fun."

"Twenty minutes and just for one." She caved. It would be nice to get to know some of the other a little better.

They cleaned up and changed. They found a bar a few streets away from where they were.

Claudia ordered around of vodka shots. As much as she didn't want it, she down it in one. They laughed as her as she screwed her face up when it burnt her throat on its way down. They started to chat about this at that. Another round of shots appeared.

"Not for me thanks, I have to work this afternoon." She knew another neat vodka would have here on the floor. She ordered a lemonade to pour hers into it, something she could sip at her own pace. They all bitched about Madame Massari and how she had made them work in the morning's heat.

"I know you work for Mr Bahar. I see you go with his driver some days. What you do for him? He is hot no? Claudia enquired nosily.

"I hadn't noticed that about him." She lied and hoped it didn't show. She wasn't about to admit to her that she had spent the previous afternoon making love with him. Let alone that she was plum crazy, head over heels in love with him. But Claudia was right about one thing, he was Hot. "I help out with his little girl. She likes me for some reason. The rest of the family are on their summer holidays in Kusadasi and she didn't want to go. Even his brother has gone today. Mr Bahar has stayed to finalize the arrangements for the party." She took a breath. "Plus, it's a little extra cash. I'm so broke."

"His wife, she is in Kusadasi? Why she not take her little girl?"

"Sadly, his wife is dead. She died a few years ago. I think he still mourns for her." She said with sadness in her voice.

Claudia nudged her arm almost spilling her drink.

"I wouldn't mind helping him get over her, you know what I mean? I would have the shirt of his back before bedtime. You know a little horizontal belly dancing should do it." Claudia was quite brazen in sharing her thoughts.

A bolt of jealousy hit her through her heart taking her by surprise. *Hands off, that's my man you're talking about* she thought.

"I don't think that's a good idea. He is still very much in love with her. It's not a good idea to get mixed up with your employer."

Oh my god she thought *I am becoming a serial liar.* She hated lying.

"Maybe, maybe not, we will see." She obviously intended to have a taste of him at the very least before her time was up in Istanbul.

Hands off bitch were the words that almost slipped from Lou-Ann's mouth. She just about managed to contain them by biting her tongue. She just smiled and let the moment pass.

Another round of drinks appeared. More shots. Oh, how she missed her cheap red wine. Lunch time drinking was never her forte.

"Drink, my darling, drink. Ypa!" She hollered tipping her shot glass upside down on the table.

"Last one" Lou-Ann insisted "Oh well here goes. We say down the hatch." With that she opened her mouth and tipped the contents of the shot glass down her throat making her nearly choke.

"Again." Claudia caught the eye of the bar keep.

"Not for me Claudia. Oh my God, my throat is burning."

"Don't want to upset the sexy boss man now do we darling?" Claudia said sarcastically.

"No, I don't." She picked up her bag. "I am going to go before you persuade me to do another one. At least our punishment is done for the day. I'm exhausted. I expect there will be even more torture tomorrow." She said her farewells and called the usual taxi company where Ahmet had set up an account for her.

When Lou-Ann got back to her room there was a small box on her bed. She soon realized it was a very expensive phone along with a note.

Thought this would be useful. My telephone number is automatic dial 1, just in case.

After spending a few moments trying work it she sent a thankyou text with a big smiley face at the end. It was quite different from her old simple beat up phone. She thought she might have to get a degree in phone science to fathom out all the icons. She would look at it properly later. Now on to her afternoon with Halise.

She would have her full attention this afternoon. They had a teddy bears picnic out on the lawn and Halise tried to teach Lou-Ann some Turkish.

"Try 'Merhabar'"

"Marberha."

"No silly it's 'Mer ha bar'. It means hello."

"Mebabaha" Lou-Ann tried again only this time miss saying it on purpose.

"I like having you around Lou-Ann, you are funny. Try this one, 'tashekular erdem'

"That's a bit of a mouth full. Let's have a go. Tshiklar earing." Lou-Ann teased her a little. They both rolled on the grass laughing. "Your poppa calls me Ashkum, what does it mean?"

"Askim. It means my love, my darling or something like this." Lou-Ann blushed a little. "I told you he likes you. A lot"

"Yes, yes you did. Come her cheeky monkey." With that Halise got up and run around the garden waiting for Lou-Ann to catch her. She finally caught up with her and spun her round till they were both dizzy. They fell back into the soft lush green grass still laughing.

After Halise had gone to bed, the evening was going to be all hers. The sexy boss man, as Claudia had called him, was going to be out on an evening business call out with an important client from Saudi Arabia. Though she would miss his company and attention, she was looking forward to trying out the Jacuzzi in her room and a having a long soak with some fragrant bubbles. The bubbles did not seem to froth as much as she would have liked. She added a little more and before she knew it bubbles had multiplied a little too much and were near to overflowing and rested on the edge of the bathtub. She played some music to relax too with no unwanted interruptions. As she slipped in, the bubbles ran over the side and escaped to the floor. She laid there in a world of her own hardly believing what had happened to her in the last few weeks.

Ahmet had arrived home earlier than expected. He knocked on her door and got no answer. He heard music playing in the distance and crept in. It wasn't too hard for him to work out where she was, in the bathroom in the tub and decided he would take advantage and join her. He ditched his work attire and presented himself naked as he slipped in beside her and put bubbles on her nose.

"Hey, you, Mr Bahar, you are interrupting my private time!"

"In that case I shall leave you alone." He raised his eyebrows in a nonchalant fashion then Ahmet went to pull himself out of the whirring tub and stared back at her. "To think I left my meeting early to come home to see you and an Arabian princess no less."

"No stay." With that he sank back into the huge array of bubbles, kissed her and cradled her in his arms in a froth scented of freesia and vanilla. "I missed you too!" she declared.

Tonight, a sensual cuddle in the bubbly hot water would be enough to keep their flame alight.

CHAPTER 14

Zak had wondered around the city contemplating his next move. He visited both mosques as if he would receive some divine inspiration. He had a few cold beers with a light lunch to try to cool himself down. Feeling sweaty, he headed back to his hotel before going out to a bar for the evening.

He found himself a popular trendy bar were the locals and travellers alike seemed to congregate. The music pumping out was mostly European. It looked like everyone was having a good time.

Leaning up against the bar was a tall leggy blonde in black over knee high boots and black denim shorts. The shapely legs rather took his fancy. His eyes moved up to her tight arse and he thought that he wouldn't mind a squeeze. In fact, he wouldn't mind running his hands all over her body and through her loose silky blonde hair that sat on the waist band of the short shorts. He got hard just looking at her. He wondered if the collar and cuffs matched.

"More vodka please!" The blonde shouted above the music to the bar tender waving a note of local currency above her head. Time for Zak to make a move.

"Let me pay for that." He turned and winked at her. He saw sex in her eyes. He knew tonight things were going to get hot and heavy if he had anything to do with it!

Claudia was not one turn down a free Vodka she thanked him and accepted.

"One more of those please." The bar tender obliged. They chinked glasses "Cheers gorgeous."

"Ypa!" She responded and they downed the clear liquid together. She then sidled off to her friend waiting in the corner for her shot. Just the way she moved fuelled the in his ache in his pants. The chase was on. He would have her in his bed by midnight or his name wasn't Zak Hopkins.

"Three more vodkas please." Zak handed over some lira and headed in the same direction as the blonde.

"Another drink ladies?" As he smiled at the girls. Time to turn up the charm if he wanted to get his end away later.

"Why not. Ypa." She toasted. Then vodka vanished again. "I am Claudia," she chirped "this is Katerina. We are dancers from Russia. You are?"

"Forgive me, Zak, Zak Hopkins from London." He lifted each of their hands in turn and kissed it like a proper gentleman. He took a little extra time with Claudia. He lifted his gaze to catch her looking at him.

The connection was electrifying. He just knew that the sex later would be explosive.

They chatted for a while him with his Essex twang and with her broken English blurred with her Russian accent. Katerina decided to leave them to it. Even she could see what the outcome of the evening was and decided she wasn't going to be the third wheel.

Claudia found Zak strangely enchanting. Not her usual pull, but he interested her and would do for some 'light entertainment' later on in the evening. By now Zak had ordered a bottle of overpriced champagne. It was slipping down nicely. Just like he imagined her body would just slip easily over him.

"Yes, I work everywhere in the world. I go where I get paid good money. I have a home in London. I love London, plenty work for me and lots of good clubs. You like clubs yes?"

"Sometimes, but I can think of something else I like to do." He lent into and slid an arm around her waist copping a feel of her firm round buttocks. He whispered into her ear. Her eyes popped with the suggestion he had just made. She grabbed her glass a swallowed the rest of the champagne, kissed him hard on the lips and grabbed his hand and led him out of the bar.

He was slightly surprised he didn't get a slap around the face for his lurid proposal. It wouldn't be the first time he had miss read the signals but her lights were definatley jammed on green.

"Your hotel or mine?" Claudia was as shameless as he was. He liked that. His cock twitched impatiently.

"My hotel is just around the corner" Zak Grinned "Let's go." They hurried back to his lodgings. He had mentally undressed her several times before they reached the foyer of his hotel. Not that there was an awful lot to remove. His man hood was ready for action.

As they reached the lift it opened and they fell in and he pulled her into his hardness. She opened her lips to receive his tongue as he kissed her hungrily. Her small but pert breasts pressed into his chest as he grabbed the firm cheeks of her derriere and pulled her closer still. The lift door sprung open as they reached the 7th floor and they both giggled like adolescents as they eagerly walked to his room over the blue thread bear carpet.

She had felt his cock stiffen as he kissed her and felt his washboard stomach against her own. It had excited her. Her own body going into a frenzy with anticipation of the night's sports.

As Zak put the key his key in to unlocked the door, Claudia impatiently kicked it open with her the heel of her boot. It slammed shut behind them. Zak slid a hand up her thigh trying to gain access to her already slick womanhood through the black shorts. They were so tight there was barley any room to manoeuvre. As she parted her legs it became apparent there was even less material on the crotch and she was not wearing any panties. He slipped his fingers into her wet flesh, as she let out a gasp.

"You're a horny, naughty bitch." He groaned into her ears. "I knew you was a dirty girl."

She had removed his shirt and threw it on the floor. He let her bite down on his shoulder as her bought her to her first climax of the evening as he continuously drove his fingers onto her. An expert at his craft.

Her knees trembled with delight.

The few pieces of the clothing that were left were hastily pulled off their bodies lay strewn in array of places around the room. He was just left in his pants as she just stood in her thigh-high heels.

Claudia bent down to unzip her 'fuck me' boots.

"Leave them on. I want to fuck you with those boots wrapped around my neck." Zak ordered huskily.

"You are a bad, bad boy Zak Hopkins from London," She rasped "but then I do like bad!" She stood there naked before him apart from her long high heel boots. It was almost too much. He slipped out of his Calvin Klein's as his cock sprang up and stood to attention. She raised her eyes brows at his tremendous hard on.

"Impressive."

He got his wish. He fucked her hard and fast till they were both sated. Afterwards they lay on the bed finding a strange comfort in each other's arms and drifted off into a deep sleep until Zak's ardour was revived. This time he pinned her to the bed and took her by surprise. She responded energetically to his roughness. Their breath rapid until they shook together with a monumental orgasm.

Zak liked rough sex, hence his dalliances when he was with Lou-Ann. She had been timid and shy in the bedroom and had had little previous experience. This Russian blonde was the total opposite. She was on the wild side and liked to play dirty and rough. He found her stamina intoxicating and wanted to take her for a third time. She happily obliged.

This time she took control, not something Zak was used to but he liked her assertiveness. It turned him on even more. His cock was already stood tall waiting for her wet pussy. She climbed aboard and slid down his hard cock. Her breasts were staring at him, taunting him. He was unable to resist them. Zak leaned forward into her mounds. He grazed her nipples with his teeth until she begged him to stop. Zac then kissed and caressed them to take the sting of his teeth away. They tasted good. They soon became attuned to each other's rhythm. He enjoyed her riding him like a cowgirl on a bucking bronco in a rodeo. He Bucked and grunting beneath her. He had finally met a woman that could keep up with his own sexual appetite.

"Fuck me! Ah baby. Don't stop. FUCK AHH!" He grunted as his seed exploded into her.

She carried on riding her stallion for a few seconds more until her own needs were satisfied.

They spent what was left of the night curled up together. Two strangers finding a strange solace in a strange city.

When he came too in the morning she had gone. He had only a few bruises on his legs were her heels had dug in and a bite marks on his shoulder as a reminder of his hot, steamy night in Istanbul with a sexy, leggy blonde girl from Russia. He wondered if he would ever see her again.

CHAPTER 15

The next day rehearsals were even harder. Lou-Ann struggled to keep up. Everyone was moaning and complaining especially about the heat. Madame Massari didn't seem to have a bead of perspiration anywhere. *She must be an ice Queen* Lou-Ann thought to herself. Madame always looked well-groomed and had a super cool exterior even under pressure.

Even Claudia looked warn out is if she had been up partying all night. She noticed two fresh bruises on her arm. But I wasn't her place to ask on how the fingerprint size marks were acquired.

When they were finish Claudia approached her again.

"You want maybe come for some more drink. Maybe some more Vodka. Yes?" Lou-Ann suspected that Claudia wanted to pump her for more information on their boss.

"Not today. Thanks for the offer but I'm heading back to my, err, hotel." She wasn't a blabbermouth and no matter how hard Claudia was going to try to fish for any juicy gossip she wasn't going to divulge thing that were not her business to tell. "I have other things on today, sorry girls but thanks for the offer any way. Rain check?" She wondered where she got her energy from. Lou-Ann was worn out.

"Ok. No problem, you choose." Disappointed that she wasn't going to get the gossip she wanted, she turned on her heels to catch up with Katerina, the other Russian dancer. Just before she left the room, she flung her blonde locks out of the way and turned back to Lou-Ann "Say hello to Mr Bahar for Me. Yes!" and gave a snide wink as she pursed her red painted lips.

Lou-Ann smiled politely back.

"See you tomorrow Claudia, Katerina."

Claudia and Katerina left and chatted away in Russian about the previous night's events.

After getting changed and putting on her pumps, Lou-Ann through her bag over her shoulder. As Osman was with Ahmet all day today so she decided to take a walk along the river. She thought it would help stretch out her aching legs. An ice cream treat on the way seemed appropriate. Lou-Ann would just call a cab when she was ready to go home.

"Oh gosh it's so hot!" She wiped her brow with the back of her hand. The air was still and felt heavy. She hoped for a breeze off the river to cool her. After a little while she found an ice cream vendor on the steps down to the river and just in time. The heat was just too much. She thought she would eat her treat on the steps and hail a cab for the rest of the way. The air certainly felt lighter down on the riverbank. But her head was starting to spin with the heat.

There were a few people in the queue waiting to be served, a couple and a family. It seemed to take forever with one of the children changing their mind on what they wanted. She felt herself sway a little. Then it was her turn.

"Water please and a strawberry ice cream." The words were slurred and barely audible. She felt the world start to spin out of control.

"Miss, you OK?" the vendor asked

"Hmmmmm." With that she dropped to the ground hitting her head on the walkway rendering herself unconscious.

CHAPTER 16

"Poppa, please don't be sad, Lou-Ann will be Ok, Won't you?" Halise directed her question to limp Lou-Ann hoping she would just wake up soon and answer.

Ahmet and Halise were sitting patiently at her bedside in a single bedded private room at the local hospital. Ahmet had insisted that she be moved to best available room and receive the best treatment by the best doctor obtainable. Ahmet hadn't really wanted to take Halise to the hospital but she had insisted that her father needed her to go and that Lou-Ann needed her there too. She gave a good argument for a child not yet six and once again her farther caved. He was now glad of her company.

Lou-Ann lay still in her hospital bed and looked like a fragile helpless mouse. She was attached to monitors and a drip in her arm. The consultant had said she was severely dehydrated and had a mild concussion and that there was no reason why she shouldn't wake up soon.

"Pappa, talk to her."

"I will try." He felt useless but he took her hand and squeezed it. He started by telling her about his day and a piece of jewellery he was designing for a very important customer.

"It's a beautiful platinum diamond ring. It has a huge ascher cut diamond and it twinkles like a star on a dark night. Each side of the mount a three cognac diamonds. The Princess was quite specific about what shade she wanted. For some reason they are not always popular but I like them. Some people call them dirty diamonds but I think the best ones are the lighter coloured ones, they look

74

like liquid champagne. This will be worn at a really important state function. The dress is the same colour as the diamonds. The ones I am using come from Australia." He jabbered on nervously. "That's were the best cognac diamonds come from. Maybe I should suggest some matching earrings. I think you would love it." A lump suddenly arose in his throat making him choke his babbling words.

Seeing her lying there still and motionless reminded him of the night of his wife's fatal accident. It was an all too familiar and painful sight. Tears left his eyes and rolled down his cheeks. He had lost one special lady and at that moment he knew he couldn't lose her. He feared the worse for her despite the doctor's reassurances. There was something about this young woman; he felt things when she was around. Things he thought he would never feel again.

Halise saw that her father was getting upset and passed him some tissues from the cabinet and tried to comfort him.

"Don't cry Pappa." Halise lent over the bed and stretched her toes as high as she could and whispered into Lou-Ann's ear. "Come back, we love you."

Ahmet sat holding her hand. He lent forward and repeated his daughter's words. Shortly afterwards her fingers twitched in Ahmet's hand. She could hear them though their voices were muffled. She desperately wanted to answer them but couldn't. The words just wouldn't form in her mouth. The pain in her head felt like she had been hit with a cricket bat. Slowly she could feel herself coming around though it seemed to take forever.

Eventually she found the strength to move her dry lips.

"Oh my head. It hurts." She mumbled startling them both and looking confused.

"Hello my askim, take it easy. You are in hospital." Ahmet kissed her cheek thankfully.

"How long have been here?"

"Long enough. Thank God your awake askim. We have been so worried. You have been unconscious for about six hours. The doctor says you have a severe concussion and very dehydrated. You have not been drinking enough water." He scolded.

She went to sit up but felt woozy.

"Stay there, you must lie down for a bit."

"What happened?"

"You were on the river bank. Do you remember anything?"

"I remember wanting ice cream and feeling really hot but nothing after that. How did you know I was here?"

"The wonders of modern technology. The police checked your mobile phone. I had tried to call you and they found my number so here we are."

"I want to get out of here. I hate hospitals."

"Me too!"

She tried to smile at him but it made her head hurt. He saw the pain on her face.

"I will get the doctor. Halise stay with Lou-Ann and look after her for a minute."

"Ok Pappa." Halise climbed up onto the bed so she could hug the patient. "It's ok Lou-Ann, Pappa and I will look after you." Halise kissed her lovingly on the check.

Ahmet entered back into the room.

"Bad news I am afraid. You can leave tomorrow and not before." Lou-Ann had guessed as much but the thought of being in the hospital alone frightened her. Hospitals reminded her of her mother's death. She hung her head and sighed with disappointment. "You need to rest now askim and Halise needs to go to bed." Halise protested briefly.

"I want to stay here with Lou-Ann Pappa." She begged. "Please?"

"Lou-Ann needs to rest Halise, besides you need your own beauty sleep." Ahmet bent over the bed a kissed her aching head gently then scooped his daughter into his arms. "I will be back in the morning after breakfast and hopefully the doctor will release you." He smiled at her with relief. "Sleep well habibi. See you in the morning." As turned with Halise holding him tight to little tired body he mouthed I love you to her. It gave her a sense of relief, relief that she hadn't dreamt the last few days and her love affair with Ahmet. He really did love her.

With an aching head and a warm fuzzy feeling in the pit of her stomach she drifted of back into a deep sleep.

Lou-Ann awoke the next morning well rested and with a raging apatite. Breakfast was most welcome. Her head still ached a little but not as much as the night before. She waited patiently for her doctor to do his rounds and was relieved to be told she could go home. She was counting every second until Ahmet's return.

He finally came about 10.30. The Hospital had called to say that Miss Masters can be released as long as she has someone to care for here for a few days.

"Habibi, you look so much better. You must take it easy for a few days, you are not out of the woods yet. I have had Zita move you out of the guest apartment into the room opposite mine. I hope that is ok. Just in case you need something in the night." She nodded agreeably. "Besides we can't have you sick for long can we. I want you back in my bed as soon as possible. It was strange knowing you were not in the house last night."

"Believe me, it was strange waking up in here this morning. I was a little discombobulated at first, at least till I remembered what I was doing in hospital."

"Did somebody eat a dictionary for breakfast?" he said teasing her.

"No. Actually I woke up famished. I had 2 poached eggs on toast and a strawberry yoghurt. Not a dictionary in sight. Besides, that would have been a little bit too chewy." They laughed together relieved that she still had a scene of humour.

"I will go and get the release papers signed. I will also get the nurse to come and help you get your thing together and dress you."

"I am sure I can manage, but ok I will wait for the nurse." She agreed without a fight. He kissed her tenderly before leaving the room. As he left her, he breathed a sigh of relief. For a few awful moments yesterday, he thought he would lose her too.

CHAPTER 17

Today was a scorcher of a day. Zak had eventually got out of his hotel around midday after having fallen back to sleep exhausted after he discovered Claudia had gone. He had dreamt of her. Rerunning the highlight real in his dreams. He could smell her sent lingering in his body. It made him want more of the vanishing Russian. Even the room smelt of her sex.

Zak decided today he would go do a little shopping. He was in high spirits and some cheap designer shirts were the order of the day. He had not packed an awful lot in his rucksack as he thought he would only be in Istanbul for a few days and would soon run out of clean clothing. He left the last 2 days clothes in the hotel laundry bag a put it on the tumbled sheets for the maid.

He found himself on the main high street with all the popular designer brands. *Perfect* he thought.

Having missed breakfast Zak settled down for a coffee and cake. He sat people watching as he let the world go by for a while before commencing on his shopping spree. At the end of the afternoon he had acquired several shopping bags. Inside were 3 new shirts, aftershave, a very expensive pair of lighter weight black trousers, suitable for the heat, half a dozen new pairs of Kalvin Kline undies, 3 black 3 white, some socks and 2 new t-shirts. Pleased with his purchase's he found a bar and sat and drank two large Turkish beers before going off to find a chemist to replenish his stash of night-time party poppers before going back to shower again.

Sometime during the day, he wasn't sure when, he had decided to go back to the bar where he had met his previous nights bed fellow. He rather fancied a repeat performance and hoped that luck was on his side. All thoughts of Lou-Ann were put on the back burner. All he could think about was Claudia's legs and boots wrapped around him while he had screwed her brains out. *She was one hell of a fuck* he thought.

He laid his purchases out on the freshly made bed and out checked out his new attire. He splashed on some of the citrus scented after shave and choose the pale grey paisley shirt. He went to the bathroom and spent an inordinate amount of time styling his hair.

"Irresistible!" He was pleased with the reflection he saw in the mirror. "Smelling good, looking even better." He opened the fresh pack of condoms and put two in his back pocket just in case they went to hers, assuming her found her. Then he reassessed the situation. "Nope better take three." He sniggered to his cocky self.

Just as he hoped, Claudia was in the same bar. All he could see of her was her near naked back and stunning blonde hair. His heart raced. Not a reaction he had expected. She had obviously had the same thoughts and hoped that he would return for a second time and had dressed for the occasion. She looked stunning, even from behind. Her blonde locks were pulled together into a sleek, dead straight ponytail that hung from the nape of her neck all the way down her spine. Her metallic scoop neck top was just tied together around her neck and across her back, exposing her wonton flesh. *Mm no bra* he thought *that will makes life easier later.*

As if she had felt his presence turned and face him. She caught him staring at her but then she enjoyed the attention. She beckoned him over with a smile and a slant of the head. He obeyed her like a little dog and trotted over her side panting with his tongue half hanging out. All she needed to do now was pat him on the head and say good boy. She rewarded him with a soft kiss on his cheek. Something else had also started to sit up and pay attention.

He knew she was pretty but now he had seen her again he realized just how gorgeous she was. The perfect piece of arm candy. He ordered some drinks and went to sit at a table. She sashed closely behind him in her high heels. They started to make small talk but the music was so loud

"Do you want to go and maybe get some supper." He suggested.

"Yes, this is good idea, need some energy, yes?" They left their half-drunk beverages and head for the door. She slipped her hand in his. He grinned a comforting smile. He knew every man in the bar was thinking what a lucky bastard he was.

They found a quiet bar that served tradition Turkish food just around the corner. It was far too tempting to skip main course and head straight to the hotel for dessert but even Zak needed sustenance.

They settled down an ordered. A huge pillow bread appeared with some tasty dips.

"Business or pleasure?" She enquired as she broke the bread and let all the hot air escape.

"Both, hopefully more pleasure than business." He smiled his charming smile knowing full well she would know exactly what he was getting at.

"So, what you do today while I work?" She quizzed him. Zak told her about his shopping trip. She agreed that the shirt that he had chosen was of good taste and she approved of his style. "It was so hot today all the dancers struggled."

"My ex-wife is a dancer, isn't that coincidence. What Dancing do you do?" He took a slug of his beer.

"Here I am in a show, belly dancing but I do lots of other dances. I can pole dance as well." He nearly choked on his beer. The thought of Claudia swinging her long luscious legs around on a metal pole was too much for his cock to cope with. It sprang to attention in his pants. He shifted to a more comfortable position. It suddenly occurred to him that maybe Lou-Ann was here to work. *I wonder, nah not possible* he thought and put the idea out of his head.

"Well that is something I would like to see." He grinned.

"Maybe sometime you might be lucky. I don't know, we see, yes?" she teased "Your 'EX' what dance she like to do?"

"She is a bit like you in the sense that she does all sorts, mainly ballet. I don't know if she still teaches." He was going to go fishing and ask some leading questions, he couldn't get it out of the back of his mind that the two of them were here for the same reason. "So what's the job you're on now?"

"Well, it's for this really rich Turkish guy, Mr Bahar. He is putting on some amazing party for his father." She saw his expression change. He recognised the name from the hotel he had been ejected from. It was still too much of a coincidence for it to be true. "He is very good looking, one of the girls, the mousey English one works for him. Think she looks after his little girl. I don't think that is all she does if you know what I mean, yes?"

Oh my God, it's got to be her he thought. He had to turn this to his advantage. Maybe Claudia could be his accomplice. Could he trust her?

"How did you get the job in the first place?"

"I just finish a job in London and this came up, went for audition, got job. The English girl got job at same time. Don't know how. Lou-Ann has no talent. Not like me any way." She said blowing her own trumpet.

"What did you say her name was?"

"Lou-Ann. I don't remember her last name. Why? You know her don't you." Shocked, Zak nodded. "I take it she is your 'businesses'."

"She is more than that, I think it is my wife. Well, soon to be ex-wife." It's now or never, he had to get Claudia on side. Maybe a share of the money would be influential. "I need her to come back to London to sign papers so I can inherit a fair some of cash. I have to still be married to do so." He went on to tell her about the incident on Sunday and how she won't have anything to do with him or sign any papers. "Maybe a little cash your way you might see your way clear to helping me."

"You are a devious man Zak Hopkins, how can I help you and what sort of money are we talking here?"

"Well we can discuss the finer points later but maybe a couple of thousand for your trouble should take care of it. All I need to know when and where she is going to be. That's all."

"I will have to think about it." She said pouting her lips at him "let's finish our super, yes?"

"Yes. Lets."

They ate the meze they ordered and drank the wine before leaving. Zak insisted on paying the bill before heading of back to his hotel room for another night of explosive sex.

When dawn broke with the sound of prayer from the minarets, she awoke to find Zak curled around her. Holding on to her like it was the end of the world. He stirred as she moved.

"Ok. I help you. I will let you know her movements when I can, but I want five thousand English pounds but you have to promise to keep me out of it. Nothing illegal. This agreeable. Yes?"

"Whatever you say honey. Now let's have breakfast in bed." He slipped his hands over her breasts and kissed her neck until she rolled over to greet his morning glory.

"You are late Claudia." Madame Massari yelled at her. "This is not good. Look at you. You look like you have been up all night." Claudia stood with her head hung low "Don't Just stand there looking a fool, warm up girl." Her thighs ached anyway, a quick warm up would have to suffice.

"Sorry Madame It won't happen again." She mumbled suitably embarrassed.

She had fallen back to sleep in Zak's arms after their 'breakfast' that had consisted of a healthy portion of each other.

At the end of the session Claudia approached Madam Massari and once again apologised for her tardiness.

"Do not let it happen again. You are a good dancer and I would hate to lose you Miss Bolshov, please do not let me down again or yourself for that fact. I have heard some bad things Miss Bolshov. I advise you to get yourself sorted or otherwise there will be consequences."

"Yes Madame Massari, I Promise it will not happen again. I noticed Lou-Ann is not here today. Everything is good, yes?"

"No, everything is not good. She was rushed to Ataturk memorial hospital yesterday. I understand she hit her head and was unconscious. This is all I know at this time. I am sure Mr Bahar will update me later when there is some news."

Claudia was a little shocked by the news.

"Oh my god." She shocked herself at how the news made her feel. Whilst she didn't particularly like the mousy English girl she didn't bear her any malice. But nevertheless, information was information.

She would text Zak and let him Know. What he chooses to do with it was his business.

When they reached the Bahar family home Halise rushed to the door filled with delight that Lou-Ann had returned safely. Her beaming smile said it all.

"Let Lou-Ann get settled in her new room Halise, then you can visit. Ok?"

"Ok Pappa." She squeezed Lou-Ann's middle with gusto and said that she would follow her to her room as soon as she was aloud.

Ahmet guided the lightheaded Lou-Ann to her new abode with an arm round her waist in case she felt faint. Or was it just that he wanted to feel her body close to her.

The room was directly opposite to his just as he had described. Her possessions had been neatly put away in the appropriate places and dirty laundry had been washed, ironed and rehung and stowed. The bed sheets had been pulled down ready to make it easier for her to climb into. On the pillow was a small parcel tied with pink ribbon.

"I hope you don't mind. I thought it would be more comfortable for you."

She opened the package and a pretty pale pink silk and lace nighty and matching kimono fell out.

"It is beautiful Ahmet, Teshekkur ederim"

"That bumped to your head has taught you some Turkish." He laughed.

"Stop teasing the patient Mr Bahar, it is not fair. Besides your daughter is helping me with a few words."

"Do you need help getting into bed, shall I get Zita for you?"

"No, I can manage. Though I do wish it was your bed I was getting into."

"You shock me Miss Masters," he teased her again. "I do too! Soon enough habibi, soon enough. Right now, you need to rest. You will need your strength for when you do." He said with a cheeky raised eyebrow

He left her to change and promised to let Halise visit once she had a short rest.

Halise was allowed to visit later in the afternoon just before supper. Lou-Ann had slept most of the afternoon away. She bought her favourite teddy bear with her and gave it to Lou-Ann to cuddle. A sort of talisman that would make her feel better. "When I cuddle Jamima, she makes me feel better so you can borrow her until you are better." Halise climbed on to the bed a cuddled up close to her side. "Zita will bring you some super soon."

"Shall we surprise them and go down to supper together."

"Pappa says you have to stay here to get better quickly."

"Oh, he does, does he? I am sure that I can manage sitting at the table for an hour or so. Will you help me put on my kimono?"

"Yes, I would. What's a kaminono?" Halise stammered not quite being able to pronounce the word.

Lou-Ann chuckled and pointed to the pretty pink fabric laying at the end of bed.

Halise reached for it and tried to slide it round her shoulders. Lou-Ann swung her legs round to stand she thought she better give herself a second or two before putting her feet to the floor. She did not want to frighten Halise by falling down. As it happens, she felt fine. No dizzy spells. They crept down the stairs and headed for the kitchen.

They were met with surprise. Zita waved her arms around.

"No lady you bed."

"Zita I am ok. I will be fine for a while."

Zita rabbited on in Turkish for a while whilst Ahmet sighed. He knew there was no point arguing with her but made her promise to return to her room as soon as supper was over.

"I just needed to stretch my legs and feel normal for a while. I missed you all and yes I promise to go back to my room not too late."

It was all agreed. Zita was calm buy now a continued to faff around putting the finishing touches to the simple meal of a Turkish style spaghetti bolognaise with homemade flat breads and a spinach, feta and rocket salad.

Later for the second time in the same day Ahmet guided Lou-Ann to her room. She went without a protest. He straightened the sheets out for her before she got back in the queen size bed that was definitely too big for one person. He ached for her but now was not the time. She quickly got comfy and he lay on the bed next to her holding her close until she fell back to sleep.

Thoughts of her raced round his mind that night whilst he lay alone in his own bed. Alone without his new beaux for company. The outcome of her fall could have been tragic. He found himself being thankful and happy that she had come home safe and sound. Life is too short to lose one person you love but to lose two would have been even more unbearable. He tossed and turned for most of the night resisting the urge to go to her room and make love with her. By the morning he knew what he had to do. The timing would be essential.

CHAPTER 18

The next few days Lou-Ann stayed at the house recuperating. She was not a good patient and worried that her time away from the rehearsals would badly affect her performance. Ahmet had told her that Madam Massari would help her catch up the following week if she needed extra tuition. Meanwhile Halise kept her company when her father was working. The tables were well and truly turned.

Lou-Ann helped Halise with her recital that was a secret for her grandfather's birthday party which was a simple short ballet routine. Halise was a natural. She learnt most things first time. Lou-Ann had chosen one of her favourite pieces of music, a Wild Rose by Mc Donald. She loved it as it had been a favourite of her mothers. It was the last thing her mother saw her dance too. Lou-Ann had simplified the steps for Halise. I was the tale of a rose growing and blooming and reaching for the summer sunshine and then its petals slowly dropping and having to go back to sleep until spring came again.

They were also working on a costume design that would be appropriate for the dance. They would have to rely on Osman's help and discretion. As usual he always knew where to get everything.

By the evening the clouds rolled in over the city. Some long-awaited rain was on its way.

Tonight Lou-Ann had planned to not sleep alone. Two nights of being in such close proximity to Ahmet was unbearable. She needed to feel his naked body against hers. She hoped he would come to her. She hoped he would feel the same.

Ahmet lay in bed listen to his own lonely heart beating. He couldn't bear another night alone knowing she was sleeping just a few feet away with only a wall keeping them apart. His loins ached for her. His hands needed to touch her soft skin and his cock needed to breach her wet silky folds. Just the thought of her was driving him wild with desire. He could no longer restrain his craving.

The door handle on her room turned with a quiet squeak of a mouse. She rolled over to face the door, she knew it was her lover.

"Ahmet, what are you doing?"

"I have come to ravish my lover. By the way this negligee looks good on you but right now it would look even better on the floor."

He sat next to her on the bed and place her hands on her thighs and ran them upwards catching the silky fabric in his hands. As she raised her arms in the air with no resistance, he slipped the negligee off over her body and threw in to the floor.

"Now that's better. You are so beautiful my Habibi."

He gently kissed her lips. And then her collar bone working his way slowly down her body. Ahmet sucked her nipples till they stood out on end. They looked and tasted delicious. His tongue weaved down to her belly button then he gazed at her face to gauge her reaction. An unspoken word was enough for him to carry on his voyage of discovery. Her legs parted as he buried his self in her. It was her undoing. He continued to nibble and licked her hot juicy flesh as she came.

They lay together until dawn sharing their nakedness and their love. After having to abstain the last few nights, the night's bedroom activities had been worth waiting for.

CHAPTER 19

Zak and Claudia spent most nights nestled up in Zak's hotel room. Plotting and fucking, fucking and plotting. Usually after a few shooters in the bar and some wine. She knew she was playing a dangerous game but Zak just seemed to draw her in. He had chinked her armour and found a weak spot and he was irresistible to her.

Some of the ideas were ridiculous. Some wicked, saying her father was ill and she was needed back in England immediately. At least she would be back on home turf. They finally decided on one plan. Claudia would play her part by luring Lou-Ann to a secluded bar they had found in a dingy dark back alley. He would call his newfound friend, the unscrupulous taxi driver. Pay him off and shut him up. The plan was flawed but it was the best they could come up with. A snatch and grab scenario. Heavily relying on the fact, she was a good citizen and carried her passport wherever she went.

CHAPTER 20

Every night after he came to her room, she spent her nights lovingly with him. They were becoming inseparable.

During the night a violent thunder storm crashed through Istanbul like a herd of elephants stampeding the savannah. Lou-Ann was quite scared. She couldn't remember ever hearing such a storm. The lightning lit up the whole sky whilst the rain tapped viciously on the windows. He had hardly stirred. She tried to hide from the storm under the sheet next him and laid there petrified with her heart beating loudly in her chest. He looked so peaceful she didn't want to wake him. An extraordinary loud clap of thunder boomed through the night sky making her shake and grab Ahmet's arm waking him.

"Askim, it's ok. It's only thunder. Come here." He kissed her forehead as he pulled her close to his body. He held her tight as the storm raged to a crescendo.

The door burst open.

"Pappa, Pappa, I'm scared. You weren't in your room." A frightened Halise ran across the room that was being illuminated by lightning. She was clutching her favourite Teddy bear, Jamima, for comfort and tears of fear stained her little checks. She headed straight into her father's spare arm as a sob escaped her little pursed lips.

"Come my little angel, Pappa is her now, you will be safe with us."

He used the word us. Me and him. A couple. She liked the sound of it. It suddenly occurred to her that she would have to explain why she was cuddled up with her father in her bed. Lou-Ann was surprised the questions went unspoken.

Halise seemed to be quite accepting that her Pappa was in the bed of woman she knew her Pappa had fallen in love was and seeking refuge and comfort from the storm.

"I was frightened too Halise." Feeling the need to say something. "Are you ok askim?"

The little girl now safely ensconced in her father's arms nodded indicating felt safe from the crashing heavens still deafening the night sky.

The storm seemed to last forever. Eventually it subsided into soft rumbles the distance with the odd flash of lightning.

The three of lay huddled together until breakfast.

A family.

In the morning the air was fresh and the humidity was less than she could remember since her arrival.

Rehearsals went well all things considered. She doubted anybody got much sleep thanks to the thunderous storm. Even madam Massari was in a good mood. The day seemed so much cooler. More Pleasant.

Lou-Ann went to the Bahar house in the usual fashion. She was even getting used to being chauffeured to and from the places she needed to go to.

The journey gave her time to think. If she was to stay here with Ahmet and Halise this would become routine. That Osman would take her here and there at her whim and that she could possibly become the adorable Halise's stepmother. Let alone any children they might have together. She wondered whether Ahmet wanted more children.

She hadn't given much thought about having babies with Zak. She knew when the time was right, they would have discussed it. She could hardly believe that she was thinking about having Children with a man she only met a few weeks ago. It would also mean her moving to a foreign land and becoming instant mother.

By the time Lou-Ann had showered lunch was on the table. Halise was already munching her child size portion of chicken salad.

Again, she was expecting an onslaught of questions from the little girl about her father being in her bed and again non came.

Straight after lunch Lou-Ann and Halise went straight to the gym to practice her secret ballet recital for her grandfather's party. When they finished, they were both feeling very tied from being awoken by the storm so they decided a little siesta was needed as they had been promised a special treat later in the afternoon if Ahmet could get home early enough. She lay curled up with Halise on her bed and dropped off almost the same time as the little ballerina lying next to her.

She awoke when she felt a gentle kiss wet her check.

"You look so cute together. You know you make her very happy." He smiled "You make me very happy." Then proceeded to kiss her rosy lips.

Halise popped her eyes wide open on hearing her father's voice and leapt up from the bed and jumped into his arms like a coiled spring.

"Get ready my two favourite girls. We are going out."

"Where are we going Pappa?"

"It's a surprise askim."

Even Zita was coming along. The boot was already packed full to the brim of paraphernalia they were going to need for the afternoons jaunt. Excitement was in the air as the headed back into the city.

Parking was almost impossible near the Galata Bridge. Its huge double layer structure straddled the Golden Horn on which trams rattle from one side to the other making the structure vibrate.

Osman dropped them off as close as he could along with the contents of the boot then went to park else were.

"We are going to fish for our supper. The storm drove huge shoals of fish in from the ocean so here goes." Ahmet handed out the rods.

"I've never been fishing before. I won't have to touch slimy worms, will I?" Halise giggled at her while her face brimmed with glee. They had not been fishing of the bridge since her mother passed away.

Most of the best spots had been taken on both sides of the bridge but they managed to squeeze into a small space to claim as their own. Rods were hastily shoved together and bait hung on the hooks. A bucket of water was filled full of salty sea water for anything they caught. Before she knew it, the fishing had begun.

The breeze from the straights felt beautifully on her face. Her loose hair tousled in the salty air while she fished with her rod. Ahmet caught a glimpse of this fair face beauty and was glad that she was his.

Zita bought out a bag with breads and a box of cheese to stave off any impending hunger.

Others were all catching their fish both big and small. Putting them in buckets and white polystyrene boxes ready for market or there evening meal. A fuss was being made a few rods down a man had caught a huge fish and was being congratulated by the other fishermen patting him on the back and smoking cigarettes.

Lou-Ann's line twitched first "Oh, oh help I've got something. What do I do now? "Ahmet help reel the line in and on the end was a tiny sardine." All that effort for a tiddler." She laughed. His line bobbed. He was line fishing and had several good size fish on his hooks.

"Beginners luck askim." He said unhooking the tiny fish and putting it in the bucket. "Barbecuing tonight."

The whole bridge was awash with excitement. Everyone was having a successful afternoon. There were fish of all shapes and sizes being landed in different sorts of buckets and containers though Lou-Ann still thought hers was probably the smallest fish caught that afternoon.

She found the smell of the salty air and fresh fish strangely intoxicating. It reminded her the seaside back in Essex when she was younger. Her and her father would walk for miles eating ice cream and pink fluffy candy floss.

They fished for over an hour after that. The lines continuously bobbed up and down. Everyone managed to catch something and they had plenty for supper and more besides. Zita was clapping her hands with delight and making plans for all the fish they had caught.

The evening ended with a handsome meal on the patio. Zita fussed around as usual and bought out the plates and a tasty apricot and sultana couscous along with a feta salad among other delights. Osman had insisted on cooking the fish on the brick-built barbeque. He looked in his element standing there flipping the produce of the afternoons work. Standing there looking as pleased as punch with himself at the finished product.

It looked like they would be eating fish for days, if not weeks.

CHAPTER 21

Today was the day when there late-night planning would come into its own. Rehearsals were done for the day when Claudia approached Lou-Anne.

"You want come with me for a little drink. It's hot today. I think we deserve it."

Lou-Ann was in agreement and was more than willing to tag along.

"Just one mind you, I have some sowing to do on Halise's outfit. More than one and all the stitching will be wonky. Is anyone else coming?"

"No, just you and me. We like best friends now, yes?" Claudia said almost convincingly.

Lou-Ann thought how hard it must be to keep friends when you constantly move around for your job. So, she was willing to accept the obscure compliment for what it was.

"I found a new cheap bar with a very sexy waiter, he makes excellent cocktails. Maybe we smoke some shisha, yes?

"Cocktails, defiantly but I am not sure about the shisha, I have never smoked."

"Trust me you will like it." She waved her arm for Lou-Ann to follow here. "It is a little walk from here. I need bathroom before we go" Off she headed to the Lavatory. She took her Phone from her bag and text Zak.

Hey sexy, we are on. She has only short time so hurry, See you soon lover xx.

His reply was almost immediate.

Ok see you soon, muchos denero coming your way. Play it cool.xx.

She deleted the damming evidence. She hoped that Zak would remember to do the same.

On their walk to the cocktail bar they chatted about what they expected from the party.

They would not get to see where they would perform until the day so they wondered about spacing and no doubt that Madam Massari knew exactly what she was doing. After all she ran a tight ship.

"It is down here." Claudia pointed down a dank alley way. Lou-Anne screwed her nose up in disapproval.

"Are you sure? I doesn't look very nice from here."

"Yes it is fine. Come let's go." She grabbed Lou-Ann's arm and coerced in the right direction.

Lou-Anne followed trustingly. There reached the bar with a small neon light above it. It just read 'Bar Shisha' in swirly blue writing. The door squeaked as they opened it. The bar was dark and reeked of stale tobacco. On the upside was a smiley young Turkish bartender that would make any woman's heart skip a beat or two. His lush black hair was slicked back to perfection. He greeted the two ladies with a beaming smile.

"Welcome ladies. What can I get you?"

They decided they would both have a strawberry daiquiri. They watched as the waiter poured and blended the ingredients. He balanced the straws the on the curved glasses. As he poured the icy pink mixture it flipped in the centre of it. He then added a fresh, bright red strawberry to his masterpieces.

There was only them along two older men playing a table game and sucking on shisha pipes sitting in the corner of the dingy bar.

"I must say they do look lovely. Oh well her goes. Cheers." They both raised and chinked glasses. They put their lips to their straws and sucked up the icy blend. "Wow you were right. It is very good."

"See I told you so. Best cocktails in Istanbul. You smoke shisha? We get one." It appeared to be non-negotiable.

Next thing she knew they had a shisha pipe being set up with the smell of sweet apple vapours emanating from the top of it. *In for penny* she thought. She had never smoked at all, not even as a teenager though she had tried but it made her turn a funny shade of green and feel sick.

She took a huge lug on the mouthpiece then breathed it out shortly followed with a coughing fit. Claudia couldn't help but laugh.

"Like this." She took her turn as the hubbly bubbly pipe burbled away. She made a huge smoke ring as she exhaled. "Come, have another go."

Lou-Ann took another draw on the bendy pipe. She coughed again and this time it made her feel sick.

"Claudia, you are a bad influence." They laughed together. Claudia's phone vibrated in her bag. She knew instantly it was Zak. A two-minute warning, her stomach rolled nervously. A second drink arrived at the table.

"I make you special cocktail, you will like it." This was in a long-stemmed martini glass with the rim crystallised with sugar. The liquid was blue but it tasted of lemons. Not what they were expecting. It was bittersweet but very lovely all the same.

"What is it called?" Lou-Ann asked the bar tender.

"I do not know, I have not named it. You can give it a name if you want."

"Well, What about Istanbul surprise or something to do with the river. Love on the Bosphorus."

"This I like. Love on the Bosphorus it is," He smiled "I shall put it on the menu as this from now on."

With that the door creaked open and the silhouette of a man she recognized. He stood there just like a cowboy in a western entering a saloon. Her heart thumped against her ribs.

"What in hell's name are you doing here?"

He stepped further into the bar and grinned at the pair of them.

"Hello dear wife. It's good to see you're having a good time." He winked a Claudia.

He wasn't going to rat her out just yet, though he didn't think it would take his 'wife' too long to work out the missing link.

"What do you want? How on earth did you know where I was?" She went to stand. He put his hand on her shoulder and forcefully pushed her back down in to her chair.

"Sit down and listen for once, I told you the other day you hadn't seen the last of me. I also told you that you are coming back home with me." Claudia hadn't said a word as she stared down into the newly named cocktail.

Lou-Ann tried to stand up again but the force on her shoulder was still present. She decided she would try to get her phone but her bag had been moved. She looked disappointingly at her new 'friend'.

"Claudia!" she exclaimed "How could you? I thought we were friends?" She chocked.

"You thought wrong." Claudia said without any emotion.

"Come ladies finish up your drinks and we will be on our way." He looked over to his leggy lover. "Check her bag for her passport, sexy."

"Zak, Claudia. What are you doing?" Neither of them chose to answer her. "How the hell do you two know each other?"

"Life is full of happy co-incidences dear wife." Zak announced. "She and I are" he paused "let's say business partners."

Claudia unzipped Lou-Ann's bag and there sitting in the side pocket was her passport

"See I told you she is good girl. Miss Goody two shoes does everything by the book."

"Thank our lucky stars for that." He smirked "She's always been predictable. Let's go. The taxis waiting and the plane won't."

"I am not going anywhere with you two. Who the hell do you think you are? I can't believe you both think you can get away with this." She looked at Claudia and tried to appeal to her better nature. "Claudia, if you help him with this you could go to prison. Please!"

"We could have done this nicely but you flat out refused. I want what's mine. I want my money."

Her plea fell on deaf ears as he grabbed her arm and Zak frog marched her to the waiting taxi. He held her so tight there was no way she was getting away.

"Ouch, you're hurting me." She shrieked. "Let go of me you bastard." She tried to pull away from his vice like grip. "This is ridiculous, I am not getting in there."

When she objected to getting in the taxi, he just pushed her roughly on to the back seat. Lou–Ann hoped the she could get out the other side of the taxi but her efforts were in vain. The door was locked. The unshaven taxi driver just grinned at her.

Zak didn't get in straight away. He pulled Claudia in tight to his muscular body.

"Thank you. I will see you soon." He covered her mouth with his and kissed her longingly. He would miss there long hot nights of fucking with his sexy blonde Russian. In fact, he would miss her more than he cared to admit. She had crept under his radar. As he got in the cab, he realized he was I love with her. But he had promised her money, not love or commitment.

Lou-Ann sat quietly in the cab. Her arms firmly fixed across her chest. There was no way on earth she was going back to London today or any other day with that ignoramus, Zak Hopkins. She would make her escape at the airport and let the authorities deal with the scheming bastard.

"Lou-Ann is late Zita, she is always on time." Halise was wearing her leotard ready for her afternoon with Lou-Ann. She was nearly an hour late.

"Maybe her rehearsals are long today askim. I call your Poppa, let him know." Zita was already preparing the meal for the evening. She washed her hands and picked up her mobile phone. She rarely used it. Modern technology was not her strong suit.

She dialled Ahmet's mobile number and explained that Lou-Ann was not home yet and he told them not to worry and came to the same conclusion Zita had. He said he would call her to see what was happening. He called her several times over the next half hour and she never answered, he too was now worried. He even called Madam Massari and she confirmed that they had finished on time today but she went off with Claudia somewhere.

"Okay I guess she just lost track of time. Maybe her battery is flat. Thank you, Jasmin."

"Please call me if you need anything." Madam Massari did not seem concerned as she knew Claudia's afternoon rituals of a few drinks when they were finished. It was not something she condoned but as long as she turned up fit to work there was not a lot she could do.

Ahmet decided he would give it a few more moments before doing something he thought he would never have to do, track her phone on his own phone. He couldn't believe what he was seeing.

"ZAK!" He swore heavily in his native tongue. "Fucking Bastard." He calmed his self and called Osman to collect him. He had no proof, but in his gut, he knew that her ex was the reason she was heading for the airport.

The bar tender had heard the commotion in the alley. He hadn't liked the way that Zak had spoken to the girl or the way he had grabbed her. He reached for his phone and called the police.

He gave a description and managed to get the taxis last three numbers on the licence plate he managed to retrieve from the ancient CCTV.

"That's all I can tell you right now." He said the policeman standing in the bar "If I think of any think else, I will let you know." He was pleased with himself for doing the right thing. He considered it his duty. It may have been nothing to worry about but it very much looked like to him the young brown hared girl did not want to be going with that man.

As they neared the airport, they had hardly looked at each other let alone spoke. Lou-Ann thought she would try one more time.

"Zak please, don't do this. This is kidnapping. You are going to get into so much trouble."

"No I won't. Because you are going to be a good little wife and be quiet when we get there. I am going to buy us some tickets and we are going home."

He had already paid the driver to keep his mouth shut. He just kept his eyes forward and never looked back at his passenger's. He pulled up outside the airport and opened the door for Zak. Without trying to make it too obvious Zak pulled Lou-Ann out of the car and once again firmly grabbed her waist and threw his and her bag over his shoulder. He ushered her towards the departures. As she tried to protest, he just tightened his grip and pushed her forward.

Their bags went through the scanners and they head on into the airport. He took hold of her again. She tried to wriggle free but to no avail.

"Stop resisting, it won't work."

"I am not going on any plane with you. You're hurting me." Lou-Ann looked around for a friendly face someone she thought could help her. They headed towards the ticket desk she saw an armed airport guard browsing around. She hoped he would head their way and that Zak hadn't seen him. Then another appeared.

"Two ticket for Gatwick for me and my wife please."

"Yes sir. Passport please." He nudged her to show her passport. Whilst he put his hand in his pocket for his Passport and credit card. She mouthed 'help me' to the assistant. At that moment the phone rang.

"Excuse me for one moment." The assistant nodded to the telephone and said no problem." Your credit card please." Zak handed her the card he was getting fidgety now. "I am sorry sir your card has declined do you have another one."

"I don't understand why that has happened." He was trying to keep his cool." He put his hand in his pocket to find another credit card unaware of the 2-armed guards approaching from behind.

"Stop, don't move." The tallest guard shouted. "Let the lady go. Let her go." He ordered. "Miss, move to the side." He was shocked but didn't let her go.

"Put your hands behind your back. "The second guard ordered. He reached for his cuffs while the other pointed his mini sub machine gun at him. This time he did as he was ordered knowing he wasn't going to get away with his plan. Lou-Ann stepped away from him. A huge wave of relief rolled over and she started to shake. Her knees almost gave way.

"How the hell did they find us?" He grumbled as they attached the cuffs. Two more guards appeared from out of the on looking crowd. They marched Zak of to an awaiting car. One of the other guards stayed with Lou-Ann.

The lady from behind the desk came out to help her steady her feet.

"The police have been following you, someone rang and tipped them off. They rang for me to stall you when they saw where you were." The tip off from the bar tender and his excellent description made finding them easy.

"Thank you so much." She started to cry with relief. "I need to make a call."

"Ahmet" She sobbed "I am at the airport. Zak tried to make me go home." As she turned Ahmet was there running towards her. He held her for longest time.

"Are you ok? Has he hurt you?"

"I'll be fine. I'm just shook up a little." She stared curiously at him.

"Your phone has a locator in it. I never thought I would have to use it. When you didn't turn up at home and no one knew where you were." He breathed a sigh of relief too.

The guard went with Lou-Ann as she needed her to make a statement about the afternoon's events. The last thing she wanted despite how much of a bastard Zak was, was for him to end up in prison in a foreign country. Though right now she thought he deserved it.

"She will do it later. She has been through enough today. Lock that bastard up and throw away the key." Ahmet was quite insistent.

"No Ahmet I will do it now. Is there somewhere we can go away from all this noise?"

The Guard indicated for them to follow her.

"Are you sure you want to do this now. It can wait till tomorrow."

"Sooner the better Ahmet."

They walked into a quiet office and all three sat down. They officer took out her note pad and started to ask questions. Lou-Ann looked at Ahmet.

"Please understand what I am about to do. I don't want to press chargers. I don't want you too either. Zak Hopkins is an irresponsible idiot, can't you just put him on the next plane home. I am not hurt. No harm done."

"What about the other people involved." The guard enquired.

"He was acting alone" She lied. "There is no one else."

The guard looked puzzled and new she was not telling the truth but without her statement there was not a lot to be done. She made a telephone call.

"Ok this is what is going to happen. Mr Hopkins will have his visa revoked and he will be escorted to his flight. He will not be able to come back either. We will make previsions that he will not be allowed back into Turkey ever again. But are you sure this is the course of action you wish to take? He can go to prison for his crime."

"Yes, yes I am sure" She looked up at the officer. "He just got jealous and wanted me back home to start again."

"Lou-Ann, he should be punished." Ahmet interrupted.

"Ahmet please understand. I used to love that idiot, why I don't know. What's more when his parents find out what he has done that will be punishment enough. I want it to end today. No big court case or any fuss. So yes, I am happy with this decision, just send him home please. That is all I want." Her decision was final and Ahmet didn't quite understand but he was happy that she was returned safely to him with no serious injuries. The guard made another call.

"Miss Masters I need you sign some paperwork to say you want to drop all charges then we can escort Mr Hopkins airside. You want us to call the police in England." Lou-Ann shook her head.

"No. let get this paperwork done."

She took the pen he had offered her and signed her name in the appropriate place.

"Come, let's go home, Halise will be worried."

As Usual Osman appeared with car from out of no were. They headed back home. Ahmet held her the whole journey. He knew from that moment he would never let her go again.

When they reached the Bahar residence Halise and Zita were waiting impatiently for them it the white marble room. They chose not to tell the child the full story so as not to worry her. But now Zak was well and truly gone there would no longer be a problem. Halise gave Lou-Ann her usual over enthusiastic hug and Zita made hot, sweet apple tea. The Turkish answer to all that aisles you.

All she really wanted to do was have a hot bath to wash that Bastards cent and sweat of her and just curl up with Ahmet for the rest of her life. But that would have to wait.

Zita was just as excited to see her home safe; she knew how much Lou-Ann meant to the Ahmet and Halise. Let alone her and her husband. She had not seen Ahmet smile properly for years and if she was the answer, so be it. The young mousy English girl had given him a new lease of life. What's more he wore it in his face for all the world to see.

"Come, I make you hot food, come we eat now." Zita beaconed her towards the kitchen. From the kitchen emanated the usual perfume of exotic spices and warm breads. A loving, homely smell. One she could get used to. Her microwave meals for one seemed to be a lifetime ago.

CHAPTER 22

The evening meal seemed to go on forever. Lou-Anne looked anxiously at Ahmet. He knew she needed her rest after today's ordeal. Halise had already gone to bed. Zita had taken her up to her room despite her protests.

Lou-Ann finished her glass of wine and made her excuses and thanked Zita for yet another superb meal. Exhausted she went to her own room. She stood in the shower and let the warm water and soap suds wash away the events of the day and thanked whatever god was listening that Ahmet had found her and she hoped. Hoped that her knight in shining armour would come to her tonight. Hoped he would come to comfort her in the only way he could.

Wrapped in a huge white fluffy towel and hair dripping around her shoulders she heard a tap on the door. Lou-Ann told him to enter.

His eyes were the darkest black and fully dilated filled with anticipation. His woman was home safe and he wanted her more than he thought ever possible. He took her into his arms and held her for what seemed for ever not ever wanting to let her go. She could feel the relief exude from his body.

"That's twice you have frightened me Miss Masters. I hope it is not going to become a habit?"

"Well Mr Bahar," she replied sarcastically "if it keeps you on your toes I might consider what other party tricks I can do."

"I do believe you are teasing me, in more ways than you realize Miss Masters."

"Now would I tease you?" She retorted cheekily. With that she released the fluffy towel which had been concealing her body. He gazed at her in awe. He felt his hardness grow against the constraints of his clothing.

"If you had left today, my life would have come to an end." He gulped. "I am so in love with you." With that he pulled her naked body as close as he could and kissed her feverishly. Lou-Ann melted into his arms and they made love tenderly until both were satisfied. Was he ever going to get his fill of this woman? Even a lifetime wasn't even going to be long enough.

CHAPTER 23

Lou-Ann had kept Claudia's name out of the previous day's nightmare. She was angry at her but bared no real malice towards the leggy Russian. Her only failing was for falling for Zak Hopkin's charms and greed. When she saw her there at rehearsals already Lou-Ann was surprised. She did not expect to see her to turn up today for fear of reprisal. She knew there was a conversation to be had but now was not the time, it would keep till later.

At the end of a long gruelling morning of Madame Massari yelling and nearly everyone else had left, Claudia approached Lou-Ann sheepishly.

"Thank you so much, I am a fool. I fell for Zak's charm and his love." It was the first time she had admitted that she had real feelings for Zak despite his wicked ways.

"I am not sure that man knows how to love anyone but I do know what he is like. He is a real piece of work. No real harm done. I am ok." She took a deep breath "It does not mean I forgive you though Claudia. You know what you did was wrong?"

"I am sorry. I let my heart rule my head, you know, yes?" Claudia looked shamefully at the floor. "I think I fell for him the first night we met. But I am truly sorry. Please forgive?"

"Well let's forget about it now. Zak's gone, I am was not hurt and you are sorry. We agree to keep this to ourselves. If it gets out you will end up in jail. We only have a few days left so let's just get on with them as best we can."

"You are amazing lady Lou-Ann, thank you for keeping me out of jail. I am how you say, grateful."

"Well let's not dwell on it and just let's look forward to the party. Mr Bahar says the party is going to be amazing. There are going to be fireworks and everything."

"You and he are more than shall we say friends, yes?"

Lou-Ann blushed the colour of ripe raspberries.

"Is it that obvious? Yes, Claudia I am head over heels in love with Ahmet Bahar. There I said it out loud."

They laughed and gave each other a friendly shoulder bump.

"Well you are lucky lady. I had my sights set on having a little fun with Mr sexy eyes myself that is until Zak came along. I think we both got more than we bargained for." She smiled at Lou-Ann "A little love on the Bosphorus for both of us, yes?"

"Hey you, hands of my man"

"Ok I promise. Truce?"

"Truce!" Lou-Ann held her hand out and Claudia took it, a firm but girly handshake. "I have to go now, I have a very excited little girl waiting for me. She has a surprise for her grandfather and we still have work to do."

They both headed for the door and went their separate ways.

CHAPTER 24

Ahmet's life had been turned upside down since Lou-Ann's arrival. He felt like she could no longer breathe without her. She had gotten a firm hold on his heart and he liked the way it made him feel. Every second away from her was a second too long.

He found himself drifting into daydreams at his desk. Daydreaming of her soft skin sliding over his and their most intimate encounters. He had quite a few to choose from their short time together but one night he remembered with particular fondness.

The night air had hot and heavy and the sexual tension between them had been high all evening. Lou-Ann had been complaining about the heat. The ceiling fans were not enough to cool her body. Even her little hot pink lace panties were one item of clothing too many. It was even too hot for sex!

Ahmet and Lou-Ann had taken a bottle of champagne to his room along with a silver ice bucket filled with ice cubes. The opaque cubes in the cooler had started to melt away into alien shapes clutching onto life as they clung around the bottle. Ahmet grabbed the largest cube he could find. He knelt on the bed next to her and let the melting ice trickle through his fingers onto Lou-Ann's flat stomach grinning hungrily at her. She gasped out loud.

"Ah! That's freezing Ahmet!"

"It's supposed to be, it is ice askim." He grinned. "Come, move here." Ahmet manoeuvred Lou-Ann to sit in front of him and popped what was left of the melting ice between his teeth. He raised his eyebrow and was still grinning. It left his hands free to tease and tantalize other parts of her body. He moved his mouth towards her neck and ran the cube behind her left ear and down her neck, the melt water running down her clavicle onto her breast. It made her shudder with delight.

"Stay there. Don't move." He ordered. He reached back into the silver bucket and grabbed two more cubes, one for his hands and one for his mouth. He moved her hair from one side to the other and repeated his actions. With his other hand he placed the fast melting cube between his fingers and delicately grazed her nipple making her back arch. A low murmur escaped her lips whilst unconsciously parting her legs inviting him in. Her nerve endings already tingling with delight, she wanted him to carry on the cold onslaught of pleasure. He took the last of the ice and followed his invitation to her soft moist folds and continued to let the ice melt over her already wet pussy. It was almost more than she could handle.

The night had ended with slow and erotic love making leaving both parties hot and satisfied.

Even the memory of that night made him want her. He ached for her. The temptation to leave work early and go home for a repeat performance was more than enticing. Unfortunately, he had to pull himself together as he had a client arriving soon. He tried to get his ardour in check.

His favourite Arabian client, Princess Amira, was coming to check on the progress of her bespoke finery. Ahmet had persuaded the obscenely wealthy woman to have a complete matching set made from the champagne diamonds from Australia which consisted of cleverly designed pair of drop earrings that turned into studs, a pendant and a tennis bracelet. Her wealth made Ahmet look poor in comparison. The princess was overjoyed with her jewellery and did not even bother to look at the end price.

"Well Ahmet my darling you have done it again, you are a clever man. Please can you have them delivered to my hotel tomorrow after their final polish?"

"Anything for you my dearest friend. Will 4 pm be ok?"

"Wonderful darling. Are you ok Ahmet? You seem somewhat distracted today."

"I do apologise Princess, I just have some pressing business to take care of at home. What with my father's party looming. I am assuming you will still be attending."

"Yes of course. My brother Salim will be my chaperone for the evening. Just try and keep me away. Our families have a long history together. I am also looking forward to seeing your daughter again. Well, I will not detain you any longer Ahmet. You go take care of what is occupying your thoughts, I here you have a new woman in your life. Maybe she is the cause of your distraction." She stood up and wink at him playfully and then swiftly left the room not giving him a chance to respond.

He was slightly embarrassed that his old friend had read him like an open book. He had tried hard not to rush his meeting but all he wanted to do was to go home to his distraction and see her, feel her, taste her.

Life without Lou-Ann would be unbearable. Even the thought of not having her in his bed tore his heart apart. He had got used to sharing everything with her. He knew she would eventually have to leave. He couldn't bear it. He did not want to feel the pain of another broken heart or the emptiness of his bed.

He would have to make her stay.

He truly loved every inch of her. He was also all too aware of the affect she had on his own little princess.

They were both in love with Miss Louise Annabelle Masters.

CHAPTER 25

All the guests arrived safely in the water taxis. The ladies were turned out in their finest designer couture with their matching jewellery. Despite the heat of the day, the gentlemen were in smart suits and silk ties and fancy cuff links. There were all greeted with champagne or their choice of refreshment. Waitresses milled around offering delicate canopies to keep everyone's hunger at bay until dinner was served.

The princess and her brother had arrived on their own private taxi and only came with one bodyguard as to not make too much of a fuss.

Halise arrived with Zita and Osman. Her pretty navy velveteen dress had a cream lace collar. It made her look as cute as a button. Her long curly hair was kept in place with a cream satin Alice band. Osman too had kept her little secret and had hidden little ballet bag and all the necessary outfits away from her father. They had been safely stowed away earlier in the day in the boot of the car in preparation for her surprise recital.

The guest of honour arrived and all the guest cheered and clapped. Eventually all were seated and a succulent 5 course meze meal followed.

With everyone sufficiently fed and watered it was time for the entertainment to start. Madam Massari and her girls kicked of the evening's performances. They looked exquisite in their white skin-tight flared trousers that accentuated their shapely legs. The cut-out sides were laced with silver brocade and matching carnival style tie tops. The dance was fast but effective. The crowd cheered them on.

Next came some jugglers on unicycles dressed as pirates. They juggled their silver sabres high into the air whilst whizzing back and forth on the bikes. Everybody was having such a marvellous time nobody had notice that Halise had been gone for too long but all eyes focused on her here as she took centre stage.

Her father was shocked to see his daughter standing there as was her grandparents. Surprise was not the word. He knew there was a secret between Halise and Lou-Ann but did not expect this. Ahmet looked for Lou-Ann and found her staring at his daughter encouraging her on in her quest.

"Oh Ahmet, she is so beautiful, so graceful." His mother sobbed "Mallia would be so proud."

"Yes. Yes, she would Mother." He choked back his tears. "But I am afraid this is Lou-Ann's influence on our little angel."

"Well then we should be thankful for her. You are happy she is here? A mother knows her son."

Who was he to argue with his mother when she was so right, as usual?

"So happy I can't tell you how much."

"Good. I have waited far too long for you to smile again. Don't let her go Ahmet."

"I don't intend to Mother."

Lou-Ann had had Osman pick up another leotard in white on which she had stich little pink rosebuds around the neckline and then they coiled down and around the sleeve of one arm and on the cuff of the other one. On her tiny waist sat her little pink tutu of which she was so proud of. It stuck out. She had added a pink bow made of satin ribbon to the back and a small crescent of the same rose to the front. In her hair was a rose bud Alice band with matching pink ribbon which had replace the cream one she had arrived in.

The music started. At first, she looked shy but she found her teacher looking at her in the crowd. Her confidence grew rapidly.

She curled up in a ball with her tutu sticking out in the air behind her. As the music progressed so did she. She grew out of the ground imitating a flower coming out of hibernation in the spring, gaining its strength from the warmth of the sun. She even managed the difficult pirouette she had been learning but could not quite manage the last time they practiced. Then with the onset of winter her petals fell to the ground ready to hide back in the ground until it was time to grow again.

She was a natural. It made everyone gulp, it was so moving. Her grandfather wiped a tear away and her grandmother's lip quivered.

Her two and half minute solo was amazing. She definitely stole all their hearts if not the show. She took her curtsey as everyone stood and cheered.

Ahmet and the ballet teacher looked at each other as their hearts burst with pride at their little rose bud.

His brother, Akin slapped him on the back.

"That's quite a special girl you have there. Brother." He assumed he was talking about his daughter but it would apply to both the ladies in his life.

A fire eating troupe were next on the bill. Breathing hot blue and red flames and twirling their fiery batons choreographed to music.

The champagne flowed throughout the evening. The waiters continued to serve small desert patisseries. They were all delicious especially the pink lemonade ice cream wafers. Halise loved these but then she loved anything that was pink. The tiny chocolate sponges melted in your mouth while the lemon cream mousse put a spring in your step. The caterers had surpassed the expectations.

Claudia came on to the stage. Her solo was captivating. She wore a sophisticated blue one piece with silver and sea green beading. She was stunning and there was no doubt she was the best in the troupe at her craft.

All Claudia could think of was how grateful she was to her new friend for not dropping her in to the authorities over the 'Zak' business and that she was able to execute her recital to her very best of her ability this evening. But her heart ached for the man she had fallen in love with, not realize that soon enough she would have to go and find him. She poured her emotions into her performance making it quite exotic. The whole audience were simply transfixed on her every sultry move.

At dusk, three men dressed in long black skirts, sequined waistcoats and red tassled fezzes came out to perform, one for each corner of the L-shaped courtyard of the tower. The skirts had orange blue and green segments on them. Each carried a flat multi coloured basket in their hands. As the music started, they started to twirl around and as they did their skirts took on a life of their own. They went into a trance like dance, keeping up the speed to keep the skirts floating. The baskets became two then four then as if by magic six and then eight, all the time keeping in perfect sync with each other even though they were several meters apart. Then the baskets were suddenly back to one. They put the baskets to one side whilst still twirling. Around of applause broke out from the audience. They started to undo a string around there waist and one skirt became two. They continued in their trance like state as the second skirt was raised up their bodies and then it was dropped into a spaceship shape. Then just as the sun started to disappear from the sky the skirts light up. Everybody clapped and cheered. It was an awesome sight.

Still they kept on spinning around and around. Making shapes with the skirt flying around the heads. It reminded of the Mexican hat ride her farther used to take her on at the funfair. The crowd was excited and pleased with the spectacle. As they turned off the lights of the top skirt, they folded it up in a shape of a baby to be cradled. Still twirling. An enormous aaaahhhhh escaped the mouths of most of the ladies in attendance. When the pretend baby was sufficiently rocked to sleep in was gently laid on the floor, it was the only time the Dervishes slowed down.

They pick up speed again and continued to whirl around and around. They released the second underskirt and made different shapes for another minute or two before spinning it away from them like a bull fighter's cape. The crowd got the feet to applaud as the three Whirling Dervishes came together for one last spin together in their simple cotton undergarment. They finished and took a bow. Everyone was astonished that they didn't fall over or appear dizzy. Everybody was amazed.

This gave the dancers to change into their final costumes for the finally. It was an array of colours from the rainbow. She was wearing the purple outfit Ahmet had bought for hers. Attached to her neck was a pair of fine gossamer Isis wings in a gold. The wings too were light with fine lights making them glimmer. The other girls had a mix of gold and silver wings.

It was a moving finish to a superb show of talent. The guest took their feet again and applauded loudly.

"Lou-Anne you were excellent. You looked so pretty out there." She blushed as Ahmet tried not to show any favouritism but everyone knew he was in love with just by the way his eyes watched every move. He thanked everyone for their hard work. As the Music was cranked up by the DJ, he grabbed her hand and pulled her away from the crowd. They past Halise who was being held by her Grandfather and he gave her a signal and she nodded. They too had a secret of their very own.

"Come follow me. I have something to show you."

They got to the bottom of the staircase to the tower and as they climbed to the top it came out on viewing platform. She felt a little breathless from the climb.

"That's how you make me feel, breathless," he grinned childishly "When I am with you, you take my breath away."

They were standing on the very top of the Maidens Tower with a gentle breeze dancing around them. He sidled up closer to her. A man with something on his mind.

"I meant what I said the other night."

They stood side by side looking out over the Bosphorus with lights twinkling on the other shore and pleasure craft bobbing around all over the great expanse of the foamy water. Ahmet turned her towards him and looked deep into her eyes.

"You have made me want to live again, not just for work and Halise but for everything. I forgot how to be happy. I look at you and my whole-body shakes with happiness. I know longer want to stay at work till late feeling sorry for myself. I find myself counting the hours until I can come home and tuck Halise into bed and then make love to you each and every night. I want to do that for the rest of our life's. Seni Seviyorum Miss Louise Annabelle Masters. I love you." Her eyes popped with shock and her fuchsia lips parted. Was he? No, he couldn't be. She knew he was in love with her but this was unexpected.

"Is that a proposal?" She babbled. Then as if rehearsed Halise appeared holding a deep purple rose almost the same colour as her outfit. He bent down one knee taking her hand.

"Will you marry us?" Ahmet and Halise blurted out simultaneously. Halise held the rose up to her potential stepmother with a beaming irresistible smile. Attached to the stem was a gold silk ribbon and dangling in the heart of the bow was the most amazing diamond ring he had made for her. She felt the tears sting in the corner of her eyes as they looked to her with hope and anticipation, waiting for an answer.

"Oh yes! Oh yes! I will marry you. I will marry you both. I love you both with all my heart."

Ahmet breathed a sigh of relief and lifted her high in the air and whirled her around on the balcony. Halise mean while cheered and clapped her hands with delight.

When her feet finally touched the ground, he untied the ring and slipped it on to finger then pulled her in close and kissed as if to seal their love for ever. Halise looked up at them with complete joy. He scooped up his daughter and the three of them lent over the railings. He began yelling to his parents.

"She said yes, she said yes."

Then he announced it again in his mother tongue. The whole crowd cheered and clapped with delight and happiness for them. His mother clung to his father as she wept tears of joy. Crying that her son had once again found happiness and love again.

Just as if it was perfectly timed, a barge loaded with fireworks began to spark. Huge silver starbursts fell out of the sky with loud pops and bangs. Rockets whizzed through the air. When they exploded, they made huge crackling noises but the display they gave was astounding. Red and blue streams of glittering light fell into the river. The reflection made it twice the sceptical.

She was so elated. This was probably the happiest day of her life and hope that her mother was watching from up above to see how content she was. She also wished Jane had been there.

They both felt on top of the world as they looked over the ongoing festivities which was now a double celebration. It was a total success.

The party went on late until the little taxi boats came to take them back to the other shore.

She woke early the next morning with a light heart and a heavy feeling on her left hand. For a second she had forgotten what had transpired on top of the maiden's tower. Lou-Ann lifted her hand to her face and breathed a sigh of relief. She truly was engaged to be married to Mr Ahmet Bahar.

"Good morning my future Bride." Ahmet said softly as he slid his hand over her flat belly. "Soon we will put babies in there, a little brother or sister for Halise." He raised his eyebrow cheekily. She responded with a girly giggle.

"Oh my god I still can't believe it. Look at the size of that diamond, it's huge." She held her hand up to the cracks of the early morning sunlight that peeped past the blinds into the room. A maze of colours danced among its facets. "I don't think I have seen anything quite like it before." Ahmet was beaming with contentment.

"You my askim, are worth it. You should have seen your face. I thought for one horrible second you were going to say no."

"I know," She replied "I was so shocked. You seemed to stop breathing for a few seconds too. Did you just say babies?"

"Only if you want them askim."

She drew a sharp breath in. The reality of it all suddenly hit her. *He did say babies* she thought. A wave of panic must have spread across her face.

"What is wrong, you are not happy, I did not mean to scare with talk of babies." He recognised the fear on her face.

"I am so happy. As for having a family with you that would make things even more perfect. It was just I had a little wobble for second. I hadn't thought about babies. We have so much to overcome before children come along. It's so much to take in." He kissed her to try to ease her worries "I am supposed to go home in a few days. Where will we live? What about Zak he still may not grant the divorce. In your faith can you marry a divorcee?

"Do not worry about such things habibi, we will overcome each hurdle as and when. As long as we have each other nothing else matters. Married or not. I am sure Zak will see sense especially after what he has done."

He kissed her again until he felt her worries slip away then pulled her tightly into his body. They slipped back to sleep curled up in each other's arms until breakfast.

CHAPTER 26

"How is it you never drive?" Lou-Ann enquired.

"I just don't, that's why I employ someone to do it for me." He snapped at her. The question agitated him. Lou-Ann had never seen him react that way. He was always kind and softly spoken.

"I am sorry, it's not my business." She was almost sorry she bought up the subject.

"Look, I don't drive. What's wrong with that?"

"Well nothing, but if am going to be living here I would want to drive myself around. I can just get a little car."

"No. No. Definitely not." He raised his voice once more. "That is just not going to happening." Shouting at her this time. He dropped his head and stared at the floor. He felt a pang of rage then sorrow. As he started to speak his voice cracked and he started to weep. "If Melia hadn't insisted on driving that night, she would still be alive." He raged still sobbing. "It should have been me. I was supposed to drive. It should have been me."

"So you don't drive and won't let me drive because of your wife's accident. Oh, Ahmet It wasn't your fault. You have to forgive yourself. Not that there is anything to forgive yourself for. You survived and she didn't. Sorry to be so blunt but it's true. It could have been both of you." She took his hand and tried to stop them from shaking. "Were would Halise be then?"

He tried to pull himself together. He hadn't realized how angry he still was at himself.

"I know what your saying is true but it's so difficult. Every time I look at Halise I see her mother. She is so much like her." He paused.

"We had been out to dinner. A truck hit us side on, thank god Halise was not in the car. I walked away with a broken rib and a few bruises and she dies with a bump to the head." He raised a hand to wipe away his tears. "And what's more she was about six weeks pregnant." As much as he wiped the tears away, they just kept on running down his checks. "I lost my wife and a baby."

"It's ok! You don't have to explain." She could see things were still very raw even after all this time. "I'm sorry I didn't mean to upset you." Droplets of water were now pooling in here own eyes readying to make an escape down her face.

Lou-Ann wasn't quite sure what to say or do. How can you fix a broken man?

She pulled him close and held him until he stopped crying.

Eventually he pulled away.

"I am sorry for shouting at you. If you want a car, we will get you a car."

At that moment she felt things change. She knew Ahmet was still dealing with the death of his wife and suddenly she didn't know where she fitted in. She also knew that Ahmet did love her but she wasn't sure he was ready to devote the rest of his life to her when he was still blaming himself for the past. Her heart sank.

"Come on, let's get Zita to make us some tea." She nodded and followed him.

The next day Ahmet came home to find the ring he had given Lou-Ann on top of a closed envelope on the bed.

He could quite believe what he was seeing. He sank into the bed as if he knew what the letter was going to read. He felt his heart break as he opened it up and read it.

To my dearest Ahmet

I am so sorry. These past few weeks have been incredible. The best weeks of my life. But I have to leave, despite how much I love you. It's been so rushed my head is spinning. This is not my home though you all have made me feel welcome.

My heart will always belong to you but I can't live in someone else's shadow. You think you have moved on but your heart is heavy and still wracked with guilt. You need to forgive yourself. It wasn't your fault and you still obviously love Melia very much. I can't compete with her.

Please tell Halise I love her very much too. You should be very proud of your little shining light. She is a beautiful and bright little girl. Please let her keep up her ballet lessons and fined her a good teacher, she is a natural.

I will never love any the way I love you my askim.

My life will never be the same.

Lou-Ann Masters.

CHAPTER 27

Homeless and out of work to employed, in love and broken hearted and homeless again in just over a month seemed to be an all-time record and an all-time low. Her life had gone full circle. Her return home had not been a happy one. Her heart felt like it was torn in two. Half left in Istanbul the other making her darn right miserable and ill. No amount of comforting from Jane would heel her pains.

On the third day of being home Jane thought she was going to have to call the doctor. Lou-Ann had cried all night until she had made herself sick.

"Come on Lou." Jane tried her best to make her friend feel better. She pulled her hair from her face as she knelt next to her on the bathroom floor." It can't be that bad. It's not as if you are pregnant. Right?"

Lou-Ann's face turned a different shade of green and put her hand over her mouth with shock.

"Oh My God. You are, aren't you?" They sat opposite each other on the tiny bathroom floor staring each other as reality hit home.

"NO. No, no, no, not possible. We were careful. Most of the time." She cringed." I am late Jane. Shit. I put it down to other things. What am I going to do?" she sniffed.

"Don't panic yet honey? It's not definite yet. Let's get you cleaned up and I will go to the chemist in a when they open." Jane tried to reassure her. "It's probably nothing. Don't worry."

They sat on next to each other the end of the bed with Lou-Ann clutching the little white stick. They waited impatiently for the results. Her expression went from a frown to an even stranger smile as the little window turned pink and two to three weeks appeared. A multitude of emotions shot through her body. Happiness and dreed.

"You will have to tell Ahmet. He deserves to know." Jane blurted out not knowing what else to say.

"I know. I know. Let me get used to the idea first. She looked at Jane's shocked face. "Oh my gosh. I am going to have a baby, Ahmet's baby."

"Whatever you decide I will be here for you Lou. Well I guess that will make me 'Auntie Jane.'"

A few days passed and Lou-Ann still had not been in contact with Ahmet Bahar to tell him of their impending child. She really didn't know what to say to him. I am sorry for running out on you and by the way I am pregnant with your child. She wasn't even sure he would talk to her. She knew she had left him a broken man. Shattering his hopes and dream into a thousand pieces.

At dinner Lou-Ann made an announcement that she intended to keep the baby. She also decided that she was not going to tell Ahmet. Jane went to say something but Lou-Ann shut her down.

"No Jane, I've made up my mind and that's that."

"But he." Jane tried to persuade her again and she wasn't having any of it.

"End of Discussion Jane. I mean it."

Lou-Ann would have to find a job and get her life sorted. She had sworn Jane to secrecy about the little life that was growing inside her. Life was not going to be easy as a single parent. But she knew she would have the help and support of her friend and her family when she eventually got around to telling them her news.

Marcia was only a few weeks away from having her little brother. She did not want to give her dad and stepmother any more stress. She actually hoped that she would have a boy herself. And least she could have the hand me downs and it would be nice for them to grow up together.

"Pappa, when is Lou-Ann coming home?" Halise sighed. "I miss her so much. It makes me so sad."

"I know how you feel. I miss her too habibi." He tried to be brave and cover up the pain he was feeling inside. "But I don't think she is coming back to us askim." He pulled his daughter in to his arms as they both shed their tears of despair.

Another weekend rolled round and he still felt lost. Lost without his love beside him. Lost in his big empty bed. His phone vibrated in his pocket.

A text awaited him

I am Lou's friend Jane. She is sick. Please come. The address is … P.S. She will kill me if she finds I have told you."

He called Osman and told him to prepare for a trip to London. He told Halise he would have to go away for a few days so not to disappoint her if his love-struck errand failed. Zita was happy for him to go and try to win her back and keep an eye on little Halise.

They chartered a small aircraft that could land in the nearest airport to Jane's address. A flight plan was filled and they were off. They hired a brand-new BMW X7 on arrival and headed towards Jane's cramped flat. Hoping with all his might that she was ok. He dreaded that it could be serious. Maybe repercussions of her fall were what was ailing her. He didn't even know if she had been hospitalized. He hoped to god she was ok. He text his informant.

"Jane, this is Ahmet Bahar. I have landed at London City Airport. Where can I find Lou-Ann?"

"She is in Queen Elizabeth hospital. Remember I didn't tell you."

Osman pulled up outside the main entrance of the peculiar looking building. He wasn't quite sure where to go. Accident and emergency seamed a sensible place to start. He queued at the window for what seemed like a lifetime. His heart raced with anguish.

Finally, it was his turn,

"Can you help me please? I am looking for my fiancé I understand she is here some were.

"Her name sir?"

"Louise Annabelle" he paused. "Could be either Masters or Hopkins."

The receptionist looked confused. But she punched the name into her keyboard

"Ah yes, there she is Mrs Hopkins." She looked at the handsome Turk and smiled." Out of the main door turn left buzz at the first set of doors they will let you in.

He followed the instructions to the letter. It led him to the maternity unit.

"Sikmek" he muttered to himself. His mouth dried instantly. "Maternity unit. Bok." Shocked he pressed the buzzer. Jane had warned the nurses that her fiancé may arrive and given Ahmet's name to staff on so they would let him in. The door buzzed him in, still feeling a little bewildered. He went up in the lift to the floor he was told to go.

She saw him. Her heart sawed and sank in the same moment. Jane's Guilty look said it all. She forgave her in an instant. Lou-Ann knew in her heart that she wouldn't keep this a secret.

He gingerly went to her bedside.

"Oh habibi. What's is going on? They told me you were here which means," Lou-Ann cut in

"Yes Ahmet, we are pregnant. We are going to have a baby." Tears of joy breached his eyes. He could hardly believe what he was hearing.

"OH askim, I am so happy. But why are you here? Is everything ok?"

"Baby is fine. And so am I. I am just dehydrated, again. I've been so sick I just needed to rest and stay in for a few days on this stupid drip." She looked over at her friend "And as for you Jane, I will deal with you later." She winked at her friend as she retreated from the ward to give them some time alone.

"I can't believe it. I am going to be a Pappa again. Oh, Halise is going to be so thrilled. Maybe a brother for her. This is the best news." He was rambling like Halise when she was over excited.

"Well it's too early to tell if it's a boy or girl. You are ok with this? I was so scared. I am so sorry."

"Well no need to be askim. I am here for you now, thanks to someone else that loves you as much as I do." He looked around at the multitude of people in the ward. "I will get you transferred to a private room. You can't stay here."

"Stop fussing. Honestly, I am ok I will be out tomorrow. Don't make a fuss." She put her hand on her stomach "Neither of us are in danger." He couldn't help but smile.

"If you are sure. I will let you rest. Oh, by the way I believe this is yours." He pulled the out the ring she had left behind and placed it back on her finger where it belonged. "Seni Seviyorum butun kalimble." She smiled in acceptance.

"I love you too"

He kissed her lips softly." Osman and I need find hotel." He lent in and hugged her. "Be a good patient and I will be back later. Thank god you are both ok. Wow that sounds strange." He left her with a kiss on her forehead and placed a hand gently on her stomach. She looked tired and pale but he knew she was strong. He couldn't wait to hold her in his arms and keep her safe forever.

He called Osman.

"I am going to be a Pappa again." Still not quite believing what he was saying thou he couldn't be happier.

"Congratulations Mr Bahar." He was secretly elated for him. It would bind them together forever. Zita would be ecstatic and the news. And he was sure that little Halise would be so happy she would sing and dance the whole nine months away.

CHAPTER 28

Claudia had returned to her little apartment she kept in London. She was relieved that Zak had gotten away with the attempted kidnap thanks to Lou-Ann's kindness. Relieved that Lou-Ann had not wanted to press charges against her. She would be eternally grateful. The last few days Lou-Ann and Claudia had spent together they became friends of sorts.

When the announcement had come that Lou-Ann was to be engaged to Ahmet Bahar she was delighted for them both if not just a bit envious. She didn't even know whether she ever see Zak again. She knew that they would be eternally happy. It had been written all-over their faces the night of the engagement and couldn't help wish them all the best.

She found herself wanting what they had. But she only wanted that with just one person. Zak Hopkins. She always thought it was not possible to fall in love so hard and so quickly. That was something you read about in books or saw in a movie. Her heart and body ached for his touch and his wicked bed room antics. She was sure she would never feel the same way again about anyone for the rest of her life.

She found herself checking her mobile for messages that never came. Every time her phone rang or beeped, she jumped with anticipation just hoping it would be him. She decided that she would have to be the one to call.

Just after a week being home, she realized that she would now defiantly have to get in touch with Zak. Her life was no longer going to be her own. She desperately wanted to call Zak but wasn't quite sure what she should say so she decided a text would be best. She just had to see him.

'Zak. I am back in UK. We need to talk. Can we meet soon?'

The wait for his reply was agonising but eventually it came.

'Glad you are back home. Can you meet tomorrow when I finish work? Southbank ok?'

They sent a few more short texts to each other finalizing the arrangements. Suddenly she felt sick and nervous. Not at all a feeling she was used to.

Her worries kept her awake half the night. She laid alone thinking about the short time they had spent together and about the feelings she had for him. Would it be enough for them to make a life together?

The sun was shining bright on the Southbank as a gentle breeze blew across the Thames. It made her loose long blonde hair wisp around her face. She was wearing a pair of tight white jeans and a lowcut black camisole top and matching black stilettos.

Her saw her walking towards him amongst the crowd. She looked even sexier than he recalled. Her legs were beautifully shaped by her jeans. He reminisced how good they felt wrapped around his body. Her breast looked fuller and tantalizing as they bounced with each and every step. His heart leapt into his mouth as she approached.

Claudia spotted Zak sitting outside the restaurant he had chosen, looking remarkably relaxed clutching a glass of Prosecco and an empty glass was waiting for her on the opposite side of the table. She tried to calm herself. A wave of lust rolled over her but today was not about sex, it was about her future.

On her approach he stood to greet her. He kissed her square on the lips. Her taste was sweet and familiar. He realized much he had missed her. It took him by surprise.

He pulled out the chair and offered her a seat. She tried to relax and enjoy the view. He went to pour a glass of wine and she put her hand over the neck of the glass.

"Not for me thanks." She beckoned the waiter." Orange juice please."

"Late night last night. Not like you to say no."

"Not really. I am just not drinking at the moment." She just couldn't find the right words to tell him her news.

They sat and chatted for a while about nothing in particular avoiding the final day in Istanbul.

The penny still didn't drop for her avoidance of alcohol.

The waiter bought her juice and offered them menus.

"Do you want to eat?"

Claudia nodded. They ordered a mixed meal of dips and breads and juicy lamb chops.

"Are you sure won't have a glass with your food."

She couldn't wait any longer to tell him her news. It was killing her.

"Zak, I can't drink at the moment in fact I won't be able to drink for quite a while."

For a few seconds he looked confused.

"I'm sorry I don't quite understand."

"Zak. You are going to be a father, I am pregnant." She chocked with relief as she said the words not knowing what his reaction would be. Tears filled her eyes with the fear of rejection.

He stopped breathing with shock for a second or two whilst he took in her announcement. He found himself feeling surprisingly happy and excited.

"Are you sure?"

"Yes Zak, I am 100% sure. I am scared." She sniffed.

"Well it's not what I thought we would be talking about today." He stood up from his chair and walked around to her side of the metal table. He took her hand and bent down to her level. "If I am going to have baby, I am glad it is with you. I'm going to be a daddy. Wow."

He put his hand gently under her chin and lifted her face and wiped the tears away.

"I was so worried Zak, I thought you would be mad."

He pulled her up out of her chair and held her close.

"It's ok Claudia. Everything will be ok. I have a confession to make too. I am in love with you. I think you stole my heart the moment I looked at you. We will make this work I promise."

"Promise. Yes? Even when I very fat?" She pouted.

"Promise" He tried to reassure her. He sat her back down as the waiter bought their food.

They sat and planned their future together in the summer sunshine as the rest of London strolled by.

CHAPTER 29

The divorce took about 8 weeks. They decided the quickest way as it was to file for a divorce themselves as it was a mutual agreement.

Lou-Ann relinquished her rights to anything. She would have no need after all she had Ahmet to take care of her. That's all she wanted and needed.

CHAPTER 30

It was time for a new chapter in the Bahar household. Time to move on and look to the future and not live in the past. The love they had for each other and their little family was strong and growing all the time.

In the nursery Lou-Ann, Ahmet and Halise stood staring down at the new addition to their family. Little baby Adam with his mop of jet-black hair was fast asleep swaddled in a fine knitted blanket Zita had made.

"Mrs Bahar, He is so beautiful, just like you."

"He is, isn't he?

They still couldn't quite believe that he was theirs.

KUSADASI NIGHTS

Jane's love story

CHAPTER 31

Almost a year later: -

As Jane stepped off the plane onto the tarmac the heat hit her like a wall of fire.

"Oh my lord, this is so hot!" She muttered to the gentleman next to her as a 146 people tried to clamber on one of the two double-ended buses that as waiting for them on the stand.

Jane could feel the perspiration instantly leek from her body and poor down her back and gather on her brow. She worried about her hair starting to frizz. She wondered how Lou-Ann managed in this climate.

She was so excited to back in Turkey to visit her best friend, Lou-Anne and her new husband Ahmet. Jane was about to get her first cuddles with their new beautiful baby boy, Adam, who was now three months old. She hadn't seen Lou-Ann in the flesh since her wedding the November before and now it was a hot, hot sultry August. As she stood on the bus all crammed in like sardines in a tin can, she wondered if she would see the delicious Bobby Bahar whilst she was her visiting, or whether he would not visit at the same time as herself. She secretly hoped he would make at least a brief appearance remembering his lips on her with great fondness.

Lou-Ann's wedding to Ahmet Bahar had been a small, civil but beautiful affair with just immediate family and a few friends and ended up with a small but nevertheless grand party at the groom's older brother, Akin's hotel. This had been his wedding gift to the happy couple. Her father, stepmother and her baby brother, Jason had even made the journey to Istanbul. Her father had stood proud by her side as he gave his baby girl away.

Lou-Ann had worn a simple elegant but nevertheless expensive long cream dress that proudly showed off her ever-growing bump. Jane of course had been her maid of honor and little Halise, her bridesmaid. They both wore vibrant pink dresses and Halise had worn her usual matching pink ribbon in her curly tussled hair.

The feast had been a sumptuous affair. Way beyond what they had asked for. Akin had ordered his chefs to make it a banquet fit for a Sultan and not the simple meze his younger brother and his beautiful new wife had asked for.

The small banqueting hall had been decorated to an exquisite standard. Swags of cream silk hung around the room with pink bows and small lights twinkled like stars. The chairs were covered with cream silk coverlets and matching pink bows each with a jewelled pin that sparkled in the centre. A single pink leopard orchid in a crystal vase stood in the centre of the circular tables and two on the bride and grooms top table. The whole thing was height of tasteful sophistication.

After much deliberation Ahmet chose his younger brother Bugra, or Bobby as everyone called him, now 26, to be his best man. Akin had been more than happy for Bugra to stand next his brother, as he had stood next to him on his first marriage to Melia which had ended so tragically.

Jane thought how handsome Bobby had looked standing next to his brothers in their smart matching designer tailored suits. She had felt rather mortified when he caught her staring at him. She could now understand why Lou-Ann had fallen in love with her Turkish lover. The dark hair, good looks and those bloody sexy eyes. All Bahar men had them. Bewitching oily black eyes that trapped you under their spell.

Lou-Ann's new life in Turkey was to start in earnest that day, she finally knew where she belonged. Jane had missed her friend so much but with the magic of modern technology the distance seemed to be less. They had managed to keep in touch regularly and Skype whenever possible.

Lou-Ann had promised Jane that she would be collected from the airport and she just assumed it would be Osman. But no. To her shock and surprise, she saw Bobby waiting at the exit of customs. Her eyes recognized the things her heart felt the last time they had met. She remembered how he tasted when he kissed her goodbye. She just hoped he couldn't read her mind. She tried to quickly readjust her already frizzing hair and hope he didn't notice how damp her shirt felt. Her heart raced just enough to make her soft checks flush a glowing shade of pink.

Bobby just stood there with a huge grin, still wearing his ray bans and his short jet-black hair gelled back into a trendy spiky style.

He lent in to hug her but the embrace was not an intrusive one. Though he did steel a cheeky little peck on her pink flushed cheek. He found it difficult to hold back on the kisses. By all that was holy, she looked so dam cute. All most irresistible.

"Hey Janey, I have got the car waiting outside, give me your bag and we will be off."

"Well hello to you to." Jane countered sarcastically. "Here take the pink one, that's the heaviest."

She held out the bright pink wheelie case with her hand still on the handle. He took the case from her grazing his hand across the top of her hand on purpose. He watched her for a reaction. She blushed a little more, matching the pinkness of her luggage.

"REALLY!" He playfully objected. "My word, you weren't joking, it is very pink isn't it." She could see that they were going to pick up right where they left off, teasing each other all the time.

"Ah ha!" Jane replied. "Too much of a man are we to pull a large, pretty pink case Mr Bobby Bahar?"

"Nope," he grinned. "come on, let's get out of here before anyone sees me pulling this thing." He said mocking himself ruefully.

The fact the she had blushed not just once but twice mildly amused him. He now knew he still could make her react to him after these long few months apart even though their platonic dalliance was one of a few short days after his brother's wedding. The last time her saw Jane, her pretty blonde hair was shorter. He found he liked the new longer, softer length. *Sexy* was the word his mind was searching for. Yes, it was definitely sexier. He though it suited her. He remembered the kiss they had shared on the day she returned to London. She had tasted so sexy, so sweet and salty as her tears ran down her checks on to her lips. He suddenly felt an urgent need to taste her poutey lips again.

He put the large pink monstrosity in the boot of his convertible with ease then took her completely by surprise for the second time today. He could wait no longer.

His hot lips fell on hers without any warning. He pulled her close as she automatically responded. It was a long sexy lip kiss. Eventually he pulled away a stared straight at her. He liked what he saw. A hot and even more flustered Jane.

"I have missed you Janey, I have waited months to do that again."

"Um, *er.*" She was taken aback. And could find no words. "Shall we go?"

She wondered if he was just playing her. He hadn't really stayed in touch. Surely if he liked her that much he would have called or something. She decided he was just teasing her and tried to put it out of her mind. After all she was her to see little baby Adam and his family and not here for a romantic interlude with her friend's brother-in-law. Though she did find him extremely attractive and fun. May be a little light flirtation would be acceptable she thought.

CHAPTER 32

The journey to the summer house was virtually conversation less even somewhat awkward. The roof was down and the wind rushed through her longer blonde hair. Turkish pop music blared out of the stereo. When they did speak, they could hardly each other anyway. She was grateful for the spare sunglasses he kept in the car. It meant he couldn't look into her soul. Just over an hour later they arrived at the Bahar's beautiful summer hideaway in the hills just outside Kusadasi town. It was a large square white house with verandas all the way round. Wicker furniture dotted itself all way round and an old two-seater love swing. No matter the time of day you could catch the last of the sun or catch a breeze from the ocean or find some shade. It was just so perfect.

All appeared to be still and quiet. She would be grateful to get inside out of this constant heat.

"Leave your luggage in the boot, we'll get it later." He held out his hand. "Let's go in and get out of this heat." She took it and followed him.

As the door creaked on the veranda, she heard giggling. It had to be Halise. Bobby let her go in first.

"Surprise!" Hallie's shouted as she jumped out from behind the sofa. Everyone was there to greet her.

Lou-Ann looked wonderful. Her pre-pregnancy body had reappeared so quickly you could hardly tell she had had a baby. Motherhood obviously suited her. She was holding little baby Adam who was not so little anymore. His hair was jet black and spiky just like his uncle Bobby. He had his father's eyes and soft olive skin. Halise was as excitable as usual.

After everyone was quickly reacquainted, Bobby went to the kitchen and bought back some chilled champagne and they all chinked their glasses to a happy summer holiday.

Mr and Mrs Bahar senior would be arriving in 2 days and Akin and his family would join them later in the week to make the family reunion complete. They promised every year to try to make it on the same day but it never happened. So poor Osman would make countless trips to the airport to collect the various members of the Bahar family and any friends that had been invited to join them on their extended summer vacation.

The girls spent endless hours gossiping around the poolside whilst watching Halise jump in and out and swim endless lengths of the pool. Halise loved the water. She was a like a little mermaid in her purple and blue metallic costume with its cutesy frills. Her long thick curly hair would pull straight with the wait of the water then as it dried in the sun it would spring back into its endless bounds of unruly curls.

Jane even got to feed little Adam his lunch. He was such a hungry boy always finishing his bottles. She had never really felt broody but there was something about feeding this little one that stirred the maternal instinct in her. Maybe someday she thought she too would find her perfect man and settle down and have a little family of her own. But for now, she would just enjoy helping Lou-Ann whilst she was here with them at the summer house.

Bobby and Ahmet's parents arrived mid-afternoon and another feast was prepared. This family had a close relationship with food. Yet they were also healthy and slim. Must be the famous Zita's excellent cooking skills to prepare a well-balanced diet.

They made a fuss over the new addition as if they had never seen him before but, it had only been 2 weeks. Halise was overjoyed to see her grandparents. They retired early as the travelling these days took it out of them in their later years.

"A good night's sleep is what we need and we will be as right as rain in the morning." Grandad exclaimed. Good nights all said they slopped of to the comfort of their usual room to rejuvenate. When the other children came it would be quite tiring for them. So, they would enjoy the peace while it lasted.

The evening breeze gently roamed across the bay as the stifling heat was put to bed. There were very few clouds indicating that there was more of the same heat to come the next day.

Everyone else had gone to bed after the poolside barbecue leaving a hot restless Jane and the last drop of champagne to sit and stare at the night sky with its twinkling diamonds. The pool looked so inviting she could not resist. She thought how nice it would feel to have the water all around her body with no clothes on. Jane put her champagne flute down on the glass topped rattan table and slipped out of her sparkly sandals. She walked to the edge of the lit pool and dipped her toes in. The temperature just was perfect. She checked to see if anyone could see. All clear. She reached for the bottom of her dress and pulled it over her head, popped her strapless bra of and breathed a sigh of relief as it left her body. She stood and stared at the pool in her near nakedness. Then double checked that there was no one else watching even though she knew they had all retired for the night before slipping off her thong and diving headfirst into the water.

Her entry into the pool was seamless with very little noise or splashing. The water was soothing to her warm naked skin as it reached into all the parts of her body. She liked the way it felt. Jane had never been skinny dipping before and thought about what she had been missing out on as she swam her lengths silently and naked through the pool. The water rippled softly around her bare flesh.

Bobby was restless in his room and decided that he would risk a walk to the kitchen in his boxers to grab a cold bottle of water from the huge American style fridge. In the back of his mind he had hoped that one-night Jane would come to his room and give herself to him. But it was still early days. Patients wasn't his strong suit when it came to women. But then they were usually more than willing. Jane would be worth waiting for. She was undeniably special.

As the fridge door lit up the kitchen, he caught a glimpse of Jane taking off her dress and then her bra. He closed the fridge door quickly so she would not see him watching her from the shadows.

He thought how perfectly formed she was standing there in her nakedness in the starlight. He couldn't quite see her breasts but he just knew that they would be pert and beautiful. Then as she bent over and slipped tiny thong off, he could hardly watch. He felt a bit like a naughty schoolboy. It excited him. She excited him. Voyeurism, a new experience, he was liking everything he saw. He felt the sudden rush of blood to his cock. She dived in the pool and he continued to watch her swim for a few minutes and decided that he would have no choice but to join her. He quietly slid open the patio door as she swam away from the building, Bobby threw his boxers on the decking next to her scattered clothes then silently dived in the pool with perfect timing to greet her on her return lap.

Jane was surprised by his presence and tried to cover up her nakedness with her arms. Within a second or two his lips were on hers. She still tasted of champagne. He pulled her into his body that was when Jane realized he too was totally naked. Her own reaction to him surprised herself. She thought that she would have wanted to pull away but instead found herself wanting to get closer to his hard-muscular form and mould her own body to his as they stood on tip toes on the middle of the pool. She opened her mouth to let his tongue dance with hers. Her heart raced in anticipation.

He broke off the kiss and looked at her. His hand brushed her sodden hair from her face.

"I am not sure if I am ready for this Bobby."

He lay the softest of kisses on her cherry lips. The pool lights suddenly turned off, turning the water from blue to black as the timer did its job, leaving them standing with just the moon for company.

"If you don't want to do this It's OK. I will wait until you are ready."

"That's the problem Bobby, I do, but I am not sure that I just want a holiday romance or a long-distance relationship."

He let her go and swam to the edge and pulled his self out of the pool with ease. His wet body glistened in the moonlight. His nakedness was beautiful.

Jane thought she had said the wrong thing, but instead he offered his hand and pulled her out of the pool then scooped her into his arms and took her into the pool house.

"Let's just have tonight Janey. Be my habibi, we will worry about tomorrow, tomorrow."

He took a rolled towel from the shelf and wrapped it around her shoulders as he did so he patted her back dry. Her eye's never left his. She followed his gaze as his eyes roamed over her breasts.

"Mmmm! They look good enough to eat"

When no objection came, he grazed his teeth across her erect nipples. She knew there was no going back now. She had served herself up on a platter and he was going to have his fill.

They woke up as the sun rose naked wrapped in each other's arms with just a fluffy towel over them in the pool's cabana.

She thought she would be more embarrassed than she was but he made her feel relaxed and calm.

"How are you this morning Janey."

"Naked and OK. I think we should go in, don't you?"

"Before we get discovered. No regrets?

Jane shook her head.

"No, not at all."

Bobby kissed her shoulders he wanted to drag her bag to his man cave and take her again but he knew she was right.

"Wait there." he ordered. He rapped one of the fluffy towels around himself and ran around to the edge of the pool were Jane had discarded her clothes the night before and bundled them up along with his own and ran back to the pool house. Jane laughed as she watched him. He looked like a tom cat on his way home from a night out. She slipped the dewy dress on as he slipped his pants on. They now had to sneak back into the house without being seen or heard.

Mission successful.

He kissed her again as they reached the hallway as they went their separate ways. It would have been so easy for her to follow him but a few hours' sleep in her comfy bed was needed so she could face the day without looking wrecked.

"See you at breakfast." She whispered as she glided into her room.

Bobby went to his own room trying to control his morning glory. A cold shower was what the doctor ordered before he too tried to catch a few hours of restless sleep dreaming of his gloriously naked Janey.

CHAPTER 33

Jane Berkley had bumbled on through the last few years. She considered herself too young to be serious about anything in life. That included relationships. Was that about to change now she had let Bobby Bahar make love to her in the pool house?

Since Lou-Ann's first marriage her mother would often say 'Why don't you find a nice boy like Lou-Ann and settle down?' If only she knew he wasn't the nice boy he had pretended to be. He had been a cheat and a liar right from the get-go and had broken her best friends' heart no sooner than they were married. The arsehole had been caught with his trousers down so to speak. What a *BASTARD!!!* His games had finally caught up with him now he was married again to a leggy Russian blonde and had a child of his own almost the same age as adam.

Jane would always reply 'Mother, I am far too young to be tied down with anyone.'

She was more used to having boys as friends rather than having romantic interludes or dating them. But with Bobby it just felt so different. He stirred her. His cheeky ways and kind, black oily eyes made her feel as ease. He made her feel like she wanted to have more like Lou-Ann.

Holding baby Adam for the first time was a wonderful experience. She felt Mother Nature tugging on her heart strings and awakened her maternal instincts. Would she ever find the person she wanted a family with? Would Booby turn out to be that man?

Ever since the little baby Adam had been born her mother's favourite line now ended with *'and have babies like Lou-Ann.'* The words reverberated around in her head whilst holding the small helpless child. Husbands and babies *'Still to young mother'* she thought. But maybe someday.

Mrs Norma Berkley ached to be a grandmother. She always wanted to be a trendy glamorous Granny. Not the crimpolene, flat lace up shoe and purple rinse kind. She wanted to be smart dressed, high heeled wearing grandmother and when people looked at her pushing the elaborate pram around the town they wouldn't be sure she wasn't the mother.

Her two older sons showed no signs of reproducing. One was off travelling around the world having the life of Riley and the other, the youngest, seemed to married to his game consol. She would get the odd grunt and miniscule snippets of his life in short sentences when it was necessary. Her father would say "Leave the poor lad alone". But it bothered her that her son was turning into a cyber junky. So, she was pinning all her hopes of becoming a grandparent on Jane.

CHAPTER 34

The boat had been charted from the beautiful marina.

Zita couldn't help herself. She had packed a basket of fruit and snacks even though lunch was to be provided. It was an inherent disposition she had to feed everyone were ever she went. What's more everyone loved her for it. She always seemed to know what to pop out of the bag just at the right time whether it was a piece of fruit or just a drink. Zita and Osman were a perfect match for each other with their gentle manner and magical ways.

The young captain welcomed them on board and suggested that Lou-Ann sat under the canopy with little Adam. Jane thought he looked like a young Brad Pit. She raised her eyebrows in approval to Lou-Ann. His paler skin suggested he was of Greek origin. His hair was scruffy light brown curls naturally lightened by being kissed by the sun and sea air.

There was excitement in the air as the yacht slip its moorings and slowly headed out of the harbour to follow the coastline on their afternoon adventures at sea.

Ahmet sat in the shade with his with wife and daughter and little Adam. He eventually persuaded Lou-Ann to leave his and the baby's side and sunbathe with her eternal friend.

"Bobby keeps looking over at you Jane. Don't think I haven't noticed the chemistry between you two. It was obvious at the wedding."

"I think you are over analysing the situation my dearest friend." Jane replied avoiding looking at her friend. "It's just playful banter." She blushed just a little.

"Well I believe you, but thousands wouldn't Miss Jane Berkley." Lou-Ann screwed her face up into the sun trying to assess her friends face. "Hmm. Just friend's aye?"

"Yes just" she paused "friends."

"So, he hasn't kissed you again since you arrived?"

"Well I, I um." Jane became tongue tied. Her expression must have said what her mouth couldn't.

"OH MY GOD Jane, he has hasn't he. Not just a peck on the check either. I can tell by the look on your face Janey." She said imitating Bobby.

"OK, OK. He almost ate me with that bloody gorgeous mouth of his at the airport car park. Oh! What a kiss. Anyway, what was you thinking sending him to pick me up? Are you setting me up with your brother-in-law?

"I knew it, the sly looks and I overheard him talking to Ahmet. Your name was mentioned. Not that I understood all of it my Turkish is still awful. Anyway, Bobby offered to collect you. Now I Know Why. He wanted you to himself for a bit."

"Argh! Can't keep anything secrets from you, can I?"

"Nope! And is that all you want to tell me?"

"Not sure what you are implying. There's nothing else to tell."

" Whispering at dawn, doors shutting?"

"*OH MY GOD*. We thought we were quiet." She felt mortified.

"I was awake with Adam that's all. I was just fishing." Lou-Ann grinned. "So there is more isn't there?

"Maybe." Jane grinned back.

Lou-Ann knew she wasn't going to get anything else from Jane so with that they returned to their sunbathing on the deck of the chartered boat.

The sea breeze was a welcome relief to the heat from the stifling heat they had been experiencing the last few days. However, it was still cooler on the coast than the hot sticky heat of Istanbul. The salty air reminded Lou-Ann of the fish catching afternoon on the Galata Bridge. She smiled as she remembered the event fondly.

Soon the boat came to a halt. The anchor was dropped. A light lunch was served along with wine and soft drinks.

After all the lunch had been cleared Jane announced she was going to jump off the platform at the stern of the vessel and go for cooling swim.

"If you wait a few minutes I will take a swim with you." Bobby said.

But the impatient Jane decided she was just going to jump in without him. Just a she reached the water a rogue wave came and appeared to sweep her away. Bobby called her.

"Janey, Janey." Bobby yelled.

He knocked of his shoes and dived in after her. He couldn't find her at first then he saw her pop up about ten meters away from where he was. He saw that she was coughing and waving at him for help.

It took a few moments for everyone else to realize what had happened. They watched with fear and anticipation as the waves pushed them nearer to rocky outcrop.

"Relax Janey, I've got you. You will be OK. Trust me."

"Oh Bobby!" She spluttered as she tried hard not to panic.

"Do you think you can swim back to the boat?"

"I think so." She coughed again.

"You frightened me Janey." He sighed a great sigh. "Come. I will stay by your side." He was treading water with her as he encouraged her to swim with him back to where everyone was waiting. "No need to worry."

"OK. I am ready."

Together they swam slowly back to the boat. After a few meters Jane screamed and stopped dead in her tracks.

"Oh my god what was that. Something touched me."

"You are in the sea Janey. He put his hand under the ocean and pulled up a huge piece of floating kelp and threw it at her. She screamed again.

"You wait Bugra." She yelled in a half laugh. "I will get you back for that you wait and see." They laughed though he knew he was in trouble as she had always called him Bobby and never his given name.

Bobby however always called Jane, Janey. She had never told him she usually hated being called that but it sounded somewhat romantic and sexy when he rolled it of his tongue and spoke it threw those hot lips of his. Lips that she wanted to kiss again.

"It could have been worse askum, it could have been a shark." He sniggered back at her. Come I race you back."

With that she pushed herself to get to the lowered platform first. He followed a second behind. Ahmet help pull the half drowned blonde out of the sea and declared her the winner. She childishly pocked her tongue out at bobby. Zita wrapped a towel around her and as usual offered her some tea.

"Please Zita. That would be lovely."

Lou-Ann chirped up.

"Are you OK Jane? What on earth was you screaming at?"

"Ask him." Pointing at the half in, half out of the water Bobby. Trying to still be cross at him.

The prankster then reached between his feet a proceeded to launch the same huge piece of straggly seaweed at the girls on deck. They both screamed again. Then laughed.

"Hey Uncle Bobby, that was funny." Halise chuckled at her uncle's antics.

"I guess I am in trouble now eh little Miss?"

"No don't think so. Aunty Jane really *likes* you. She won't be mad for long."

By now he had pulled his well-polished form on the deck. Jane was waiting for him to find her on the inner sanctum of the boat. Instinctively she just knew he would come to her.

"So, where is she?

Halise pointed the way.

"Thanks baby girl."

Jane sat with the wet towel around her sipping her hot apple tea. As he entered still in his dripping wet shorts, she looked bravely into his eyes. Those deep black eyes. They looked deeper than the ocean that was tapping gently on the side of the boat.

"Thank you for saving me."

God!! He looked like an Adonis standing there. It made it hard for her to concentrate. She felt her nipples rise against her wet bikini but it wasn't the cold that had made them erect.

"No problem Janey. I wasn't going to let the most beautiful girl on the boat drown, was I?" He couldn't take his eyes of her. "You scared me half to death askim when I couldn't find you. You scared us all in fact. Good job you are a strong swimmer otherwise who knows. Those rocks could have been a real problem." He took a few steps towards her. He felt the need to kiss her and hold her safe in his muscular arms. His lips were just about to descend up hers.

"Hey you guys, all OK now?" Lou-Ann came busting in with little Adam in her arms.

They both looked sheepishly at her. Lou-Ann realised she had appeared at an inopportune moment. Her suspicions were confirmed. There was definitely something going on between them.

"*OOPPSS!*" She blushed a little herself. "Sorry just checking up on you. But I see you are obviously in fine hands *Janey.*" Lou-Ann couldn't help a little sarcasm. Jane pursed her lips together scowled at her.

"I am, erm, that is, we are both OK Lou-Ann." Jane announced slightly mortified as she had only just tried denied anything was going on between her and the youngest Bahar brother. Bobby still was looking at his Janey as he stepped back. "Could you send Halise down with my bag Bobby, I would like to change please."

He felt like he was being dismissed like a petulant child. If only his brother's wife hadn't appeared at that moment, he would have been able to steel yet another kiss from the beautiful blonde. *She must realize that I have feelings for her by now* he thought as he climbed up to the top deck were Halise was chatting to her father about her brave uncle and his rescuing the fair maiden.

"It was like out a story book Pappa. It was like he was rescuing a mermaid with long golden hair." Typical of Halise to over dramatize things. Though Ahmet could see where she was coming from.

"Yes, your Uncle is very brave."

"Oh, I am sorry for bursting in on you I just didn't think." Lou-Ann put her hand over her mouth when Jane flushed a little pinker than usual. "OH MY! Jane Berkley! You are falling for him, aren't you? He was just about to kiss you wasn't he." Flames now run up Jane's face.

"Yes! and Yes! You should have warned me about him. It's just harmless flirting. A little fun. But by god he has an amazing body."

"They all have and don't tell Ahmet I said that." They both sniggered.

"Auntie Jane you OK? What's so funny?" Halise came down clutching Jane's colourful beach bag. She was almost glad of the excuse to get Bobby out of way. She wasn't sure what would have happened if they had not been interrupted. She didn't trust herself with him especially in confined spaces and not wearing much. She reached into the bag and grabbed a dry bikini.

"Nothing darling, we were just laughing about the seaweed."

Halise handed the bag to Jane.

"Uncle Bobby did that because he likes you." She turned on her heels and headed back up the stairs humming to herself. Both of them bust out laughing again.

"Perceptive little thing isn't she."

"That she is Jane. Hurry up and get changed, I'll see you up on deck."

"OK. I will be two minutes."

Jane riffled through her bag found her dry, unsalted bikini. She changed as quickly as she could. Reapplied her sunscreen and headed up top. Bobby watched her as she purposely minced passed him. She gave him a devil may care glance.

The captain announced he was pulling up the anchor and setting sail back to the port of Kusadasi.

His soul burned for her. *Dam Lou-Ann for bursting in on us.* Bobby thought as the blood heated in his veins. For the rest of the afternoon he would have to try to avoid direct eye contact with the bewitching Jane. Her sexy, slim figure in her string bikini was making his blood rush south. He was grateful for loose swim shorts that hid his stirrings.

His thoughts were suddenly distracted as Zita shouted to Halise.

"Yunus, yunus. Halise look quick."

"Dolphins" Hallies translated.

Everyone rushed to the front of the boat as a small pod of silvery grey Bottle nose Dolphins appeared and started to glide through the bowl waves. They went from 3 then to 4 then they seem to be about

8 dancing in through the bubbles in the waves having their own family afternoon adventure.

"Pappa, Pappa. Look at the baby one he is so tiny just like baby Adam."

Her Pappa grinned and leant over and kissed his little girl then put his arm around his wife who was holding his son. A perfect little family. He thought it was hard to believe that just over a little over a year ago he was a heart broken man living a life of regrets and torment. Lou-Ann had come into his life and mended his shattered heart and glued all the pieces of it back together with her constant love.

"He is tiny, isn't he? See how close he stays to his Mamma."

"Just like Adam." Halise announced.

"Just like Adam!" Her Pappa repeated.

Two other dolphins kept flipping out of the water and made a splashing sounds every time they gracefully re-entered the water. The largest of the group was a show off. He spiralled himself high into the air before he too dived back in crystal blue ocean. It was like a synchronised Dolphin swim team as they played in the foam leaping this way and that. Halise clapped her hand with excitement as Jane tried to capture the event on her little camera.

Everyone was in awe of the magical creatures. They oooed and aahhed as they continued to play alongside the vessel.

The silvery creatures continued to put on the perfectly choreographed show for about twenty minutes. As quickly as they arrived, they vanished.

They chatted about the event on the way back to port. Halise saying did you see this and did see you that.

When shoreline was insight Bobby caught Jane staring out to sea. She had put a cover up on but it wafted gently around her as an early evening breeze rose up to greet them back as they headed back to port, Jane was leaning over the railings looking bemused. Everyone else had gone below deck to sort out their belongings for disembarkation. He couldn't avoid her any longer. He sidled alongside her. He playfully bumped her hip with his.

"Hey you."

"Hey you."

"I am sorry I was so … forward earlier. I was just glad that you were OK."

"MY HERO!" She exclaimed. "It's OK. We just got caught up in the moment. Let's not worry about it."

"So, if I was to put my arm around you would you mind?"

"No. No I wouldn't mind. In fact, I think I might quite like." She grinned inwardly to herself.

He gently placed his arm her shoulder as they continued to stare silently at the ocean.

Bobby's inner boy smiled secretly to himself. Pleased with his accomplishment. He liked the way she felt close by his side. At least he now knew she reciprocated his feelings even if it was just a fraction of what he was feeling for her right now. It was a good place start. He hadn't wasted those nights dreaming of the pretty English blonde wearing the bright pink bridesmaid dress. The few days they had spent together then was just a flirtatious crush or so he thought. That was until he saw her again when he collected her at the airport. He had just over two weeks to declare his hand and his growing love. But right now, he had to cool his ardour.

The cat was truly out of the bag. Ahmet and Lou-Ann had left the children on the lower deck with Zita when they saw Bobby and Jane in close proximity to each other. Lou-Ann nudged her husband's arm.

"Young love." She whispered.

"I thought he has been acting strange."

"I kind of interrupted them earlier. I think he was about to kiss her."

"Oh. He is a dark horse. He is also a player."

"Harmless fun Jane called it. I think it is a lot more. She looks smitten to me."

They crept back down below without disturbing the couple. They left them there until they had nearly docked. By time everyone was back on deck they had parted, thinking that no one but them knew about his affair with Lou-Ann's best friend.

"Do you remember the moment when you fell in love with me?" She asked her husband.

"I do indeed. The moment was when we stood looking out over the river with Halise the first day you came to the house."

CHAPTER 35

Bobby had secretly organised a romantic soiree just for the two of them. It had been difficult even almost impossible for them to truly have a moment to themselves since the rest of the family arrived. Four more Adults and three young children. Nobody was getting any peace or quiet. Tonight, it was just going to be himself and Jane and the waiter and he had another surprise in store later if the evening was successful.

Bobby had left a little earlier than Jane. Osman had been kind enough to agree to make the trip twice. He had wanted to make sure that the scene was set and that everything was perfect for his Janey. HIS JANEY. No one else's, just his. The blond English girl had truly gotten under his olive skin.

Jane faffed around trying keep herself calm and her nerves it check. She wasn't quite sure why she was feeling the way she was. Her tummy all butterflies and her heart racing. She didn't want to appear as if she was trying too hard. She had already changed her outfit 3 times. She felt like Bridget Jones in a film she once watched were her entire wardrobe had been unsuccessfully tried and flung on the bed on trying to find the right attire for the occasion. She eventually settled on a long flowing thin strapped sundress that crossed over the in the back leaving her shoulders exposed. The print was of delicate rosebuds on a cream background.

Lou-Ann had curled Janes hair in soft blonde waves that fell loosely to her shoulders. Her makeup was soft and subtle. Finished to perfection with a pale coral lip gloss with a hint of gold flakes. This was her prize possession in her entire meagre make-up collection. She purchased it on a whim and it had been far too expensive. But the girl on the make-up counter in her local department store had promised it would suit her down to the ground and would be good for all occasions, albeit night or day, work or out on a date. She had begrudgingly handed over her £28 on went on her way. As it now seems the shop girl was right. It picked up the tones in her delicate English complexion that now had a light tan. She chose a sparkly pair of thong sandals with a small kitten heel. Then to top it off, Lou-Ann lent her a little bag and wrap.

"Oh Jane! You look so pretty. Out to catch a big fish tonight, are we?"

"Behave Jane, it is just dinner. Besides I think I am the one who has already been hooked!!"

"Jane Berkley! Are you saying what I think you are saying?"

"Oh Lou-Ann. I am not sure! Maybe I am just a little head over heels for him. It is supposed to be a little fun, a holiday fling. But I fear it may be more."

It almost felt like a confession.

"Well you hang on to your heart just a little longer. You Know Bobby is a bit of a player. Don't get hurt Jane." She smiled. "But you should however have a bit of fun. Ahmet says Bobby is smitten with you too! He says he has never seen him like this before."

At that moment the car beeped to signal its return to take her to 'the secret location'. She looked in the mirror one last time. She like the reflection that was staring back at her. It was not her usual jeans and baggy top. It was a sophisticated young woman with love, even lust on her mind.

"Perfect. Now go Jane, go and enjoy your evening at stop worrying. At least it will be peaceful with no kids making a raucous." She lent in and hugged her stunningly dressed dearest friend and headed for were the car was parked. She could feel the nerves jangling in the pit of her stomach. *What if he was a player? Tonight, he is mine.* she thought.

Osman did his usual ritual of opening the car door and making sure his special passenger was safely on board. He grinned oddly at her. He knew the spot well. He taken Zita there once before on her birthday and he felt them fall in love all over again on the idyllic spot.

It would take about 25 minutes to get the cove. Her heart raced a little more than usual. She wasn't sure if it was just excitement or the lusty thoughts that kept creeping into her subconscious. The memories of they had made love in the pool house made her stir in unfathomable ways. Almost uncomfortably. She hoped that Osman didn't know what she was thinking.

Osman drove most of the way in silence with his face a grin with his own private thought of the so romantic, so special secret place.

The car came to stop down a pine filled gravelled lane. Osman jumped out to open the door but Jane still unaccustomed to his habits beat him to it. Though when he held his hand out to help her escape the metal box on wheels, she gratefully obliged. A middle-aged man dressed in a smart black waistcoat and a matching black bow tie was waiting for her at the top of a zigzag shape run of jagged steps. He held out a glass of refreshing lemony fizz to quench her thirst. She took a sip so not to appear rude and put in back on the silver tray. He showed her to the steps

"This way Miss Jane. Mr Bahar is waiting for you at the bottom."

She looked at the stairs with trepidation, now thankful for choice of flatter sandals. She hoped to make her entrance at the bottom an elegant one. Not one of a clumsy buffoon falling all over the place. She sighed with relief as the seemingly endless steps became three, then two and finally one. There she stared straight into Booby's eyes as he held his hand like an old-fashioned gentleman waiting for his Lady. He kissed her gently on both checks. Though he would have like more, much more, but he wanted this evening to more than about lust and sex. He wanted to romance her and make her feel special.

As he held her hand, she felt like Cinderella being led away by her own handsome Prince Charming. He led her to a small rocky outcrop which had a small intimate table set for two. With several Turkish glass lanterns hanging on metal rods adding to the ambience.

The sun was still quite high in the sky surrounded by a few faint wispy clouds. Soon it would start lowering itself to bed. Leaving the sky streaked with vivid reds and purples.

He pulled out the chair as she went to sit, he put it underneath her in the perfect position so she would sit on the padded cushion that covered the metal seat. On the table was a silver bucket filled with ice and in it a bottle of the finest Bollinger that had been strategically placed. The cutlery shone in the slowly disappearing evening sunlight.

Bobby sat opposite her with his eyes hardly ever leaving her gaze.

"I hope you like the food I have chosen for us evening, unfortunately due to its remote location it has to be pre-ordered."

The waiter that accompanied her down the stairs approached and as Bobby nodded, he took the chilled champagne from the bucket and begun the technical proses of its opening. Then with a large pop and very little waste is was ready to poor.

Jane nodded a silent 'yes please' to the man.

"I am sure you have impeccable taste Mr Bahar." A small puff of wind blew over the table threatening to mess with her new wavy hair do but it dissipated quickly.

"I am sure of it". He said cockily "Otherwise you would not be sitting here with me." Jane blushed. "May I say you are looking stunning this evening Janey."

"Thank you and you look very dashing yourself."

He had kept it quite casual with his designer jeans and a navy Armani jacket with a crisp white shirt unbuttoned just enough to see his dark hairy chest. It made her quiver just ever so slightly. Her nerves fluttered again.

As they ate there starters of calamari and delicious flat breads the sun started its bedtime routine. The bright orange red ball fell closer into the sea. The waves lapped against the rocks with their soft white meringue peaks.

By the time main dish was served the sky had turned a clash of colours. The waiter had bought up the entrée on a volcanic hot plate. The meat almost raw. The worst thing possible for Jane. But felt she couldn't complain. Bobby must have seen her turn her nose up.

"Its OK askum, it carries on cooking on the hot stones."

The sun in her wisdom was putting on an extravagant display especially for the two lovers whilst they were having their romantic liaison. The lower the flaming ball got the ocean the more the colours changed. Red to pink to purple. Just as the meal was ending, he took her hand.

"Watch this."

She turned her head to see the sun almost gone. It was the most amazing sunset she could recall ever seeing.

"THREE, TWO, ONE. Gone." Gone for the night to rest for the next day, to be replaced with a purplish grey sky that waited to turn black so the stars could come out to play.

"Wow. That was breath taking. Thank you for bringing me here. It is a stunning location how did you know about it."

"Believe it or not Osman. He bought his wife here a few years ago for a special occasion."

"Ah yes, the magical Osman. Lou-Ann has told me he apparently knows how and where to get almost anything."

"He is a man of many talents. Oh, and his wife, Zita's cooking is some of the best food you could ever taste." He stood pulled her to her feet and pulled her to him. "Talking of tasting ..." He lowered his mouth over hers. Hungrily, greedily parting her lips with his tongue. She could not help herself. Jane moved herself closer and kissed him Just as fervently back.

The passion ignited by that kiss was not to be resolved there and then. He wanted to take her right there and by the way she had kissed him back she felt the same. As they pulled away breathlessly away from their steamy embrace he apologised for his eagerness.

"I find it very hard to control myself when you are around, I am sorry!"

"Please stop saying sorry. If I hadn't wanted you to kiss me you would have, believe me." She lent her forehead against his. "I have waited for a kiss like that all my life and I am glad it was you who provided it." The next kiss was more tender and softer. Nipping at her lower lip. Stirring his ardour once again. She felt the movement in his boxers and wished she could have a few private moments to help release his tension.

As the sky went black a small vessel with a light approached.

"AH! The second part of the evening is about to arrive. Are you going to be ok going on another boat? I gave Osman the rest of the night off and chartered a boat to take us back."

"I am sure I will be just fine."

He thanked the waiter and told him to thank his staff for providing their service. Bobby the pushed a couple of 100 lira notes in the older man's hands. He nodded and appeared most grateful.

"Follow me and be careful. I promise I will catch you." Jane looked speculatively at the gap between the rocks and vessel. "Trust me."

"Ok. I do trust you."

Bobby climbed down some old rickety steps and jump on board the pleasure cruiser.

Jane gingerly followed and held her hand out and jumped and as promised landed her safely aboard the vessel.

"Thank the lord for that. Thanks Bobby."

"Your welcome. I am just grateful that the water is so very calm tonight and you didn't fall in again. I am wearing Armani you know?"

She pushed him playfully away. But he pulled her back into his arms and moved her to the safety of the centre of the boat. He put his hand up to her face and moved her blond locks of her face before he stole another cheeky kiss.

"You certainly know how to sweep a poor innocent girl off her feet."

"NOT so innocent I think."

The boat revved up its engine and started slowly out to head back out to sea.

"We have several options. We can go back it will take about 45 mins to cruise to the harbour or take a long cruise or" He raised his eyebrows "we can stay out all night. What do you think to that little Miss innocent?"

"Bugra Bahar. I think you are being far too presumptuous. What makes you think for one minute I would spend the whole night with you on this boat?"

"OK, I will tell the skipper to take us back straight away." His response was quick and nonchalant.

"Let's not be too hasty, maybe we can take option 2 and cruise for a while."

Bobby shouted instructions at the skipper in Turkish. He could have said anything to him and she didn't care as long as she got some *'alone'* time with Bobby. The secret idyllic location was not the only secret spot she wanted to share with him tonight. She really wanted to tell him that option three would be more to her liking but did not want to appear to wanton or desperate for his magical touch.

"Now you are making sense." He stepped down into the galley and shouted back up "Do you want some more champagne askim? Or something else?"

"Something else."

She turned on her heels hitched her long flowing dress up and climbed down the short ladder to were Bobby was standing. He watched her every move. He watched her buttocks as they swayed from side to side as she descended backwards into the cabin.

"And what would that something else be?" as she turned at met his gaze.

"YOU!!" She let out a soft sigh that was the start of her seduction. She felt extremely aware that there was someone else aboard and in quite close proximity. But this made it even more thrilling. Naughty even.

She tenderly kissed his lips and he laid his hands on her shoulders and then continued to run them down to the buttocks he had just been admiring.

"Kıçına seviyorum"

She wasn't sure what he said but she had a vague idea judging were his hands were. He nuzzled into her neck. She smelt of a delicate perfume and sea breeze. The heady mixture excited him. She could feel his warm breath as he spoke softly "Are you sure you want this my Janey."

She pulled away from him ever so slightly, he had a look of confusion on his face. For one split second he thought she was about to change her mind. Their eyes locked and they both knew what was about to happen. His cock stiffened with the promise of pleasure. It ached for release from the confines of his designer underpants.

She let the straps of her dress drop off her shoulders as seductively as was possible. It was just loose enough for it to slide down her slender body with a little shimmy to help it along its way.

"I want to thank you for this evening." She stood before him in the tiniest white thong and a matching strapless bra were erect nipples were straining to escape their demi cups. She pushed him on to the tan leather seating and straddled him. For a woman of little experience, she appeared to know exactly what she was doing. Jane had seen enough films to know what a seduction should look like.

With his mouth found her pink rose buds as he tenderly at first kissed and caressed them through the fabric. She could feel his erection between her legs growing ever harder. He still sat fully clothed. It was to restricting and begged her to remove his jacket. She slid it of his shoulders at left it in a crumpled heap behind him. Next his shirt was off and it joined the jacket. His hands found her arse. He squeezed it tightly, almost painfully. She reached behind and unclipped her bra and released her breast from their restraints. This time Bobby was not so gentle in his foreplay. His mouth tugged and pulled hard on her exposed buds which nearly took her to the brink of no return.

Breathlessly she raised herself from his lap. She wanted what was hers, what was waiting for her in his tight bulging jeans. They too were soon discarded, as was the prison in which his throbbing manhood was held. He slid to his knees and look at her secret place which the thong was still keeping him from having access to. He kissed the top then her inner thigh. Then slowly slide the thin piece of material down her thighs to the floor.

He encouraged her to part her legs a little more whilst he brushed his nose across her public hair. Her soft blonde curly hair. Her sent let him know she was ready for him. To steady herself she had to rest her hands on his shoulders. Then it happened. His tongue darted into her sex. It was more than she could bear. Her legs shook and started to give way within seconds. His knowing tongue was her undoing.

He scooped up the quivering blonde and took her to the small cabin and made her world shake violently again until he could no longer stave off his own ejaculation. They lay twisted together like a love knot for what seemed like an age. Breathing erratically but certainly sated. Eventually dozed off curled together in a gratified sleep with the gentle rocking of the vessel to aid them.

In the early hours Jane awoke startled. She had almost forgotten where she was and who she was with. With sigh of relief she hadn't dreamt the whole thing, she snuck out to find the small bathroom. A she looked in the mirror on the back of the door she saw a more mature, a more complete Jane staring back at her. As she sat to pee, I suddenly hit her they had not used any contraception in the heat of the moment.

"OH SHIT, SHIT, SHIT." She exclaimed to herself hoping that Bobby hadn't heard her. She gathered herself together then went back to bedroom. To her surprise Bobby was sat up in bed awaiting her return.

"I thought you may have fallen overboard again." He said sarcastically. "Are you ok habibi? I heard you in the bathroom, the walls are quite thin."

"In our haste we forgot to use a condom Bobby. What if …?"

"I am sure you will be fine. But if not I will run away with you and our beautiful unborn child and marry you and then keep you bare foot and pregnant forever." He replied unperturbed.

"Pregnant forever I think not, maybe just once or twice. My mother would be overjoyed." Jane Joked. Her mood suddenly changed. "Seriously, it scares me. We have already complicated the hell out of, well whatever this is." She let out a small rye laugh. "I am not ready to become a mother. It suites Lou-Ann but me, I am not so sure."

"Someday you will make a beautiful mother and you will make your own mother a proud grandmother. Do not worry for now." He gave her an encouraging smile. His eyes glanced down to his awakening manhood and raised an eyebrow evocatively. "Come back to bed my askim. Tonight we can just enjoy each other, then tomorrow we will worry."

Jane half wished she could find a reason to reject his ever-growing offer. But the damage had possibly already been done. She suggestively crawled over the white sheets that had been strewn across the cabins bed. She straddled his awaiting hardness where he gratefully received her.

The alarm woke them abruptly. Jane stretched her content but slightly sore body and then rolled into bobby's awaiting arms. He too was wide awake now.

"What time is it Bobby? I am still so tired."

He raised an eyebrow.

"I am not surprised. Time to get up. Grab the sheet. And we shall go on deck."

She did as he asked. she grabbed the sheet from the bed and managed to make a sarong out of it. Pleased with her effort she followed her lover to the galley. He open the door to go out on deck and it was still pitch black. A few stars still twinkled in the early morning sky.

"Just wait a few minutes and you shall see." They stood and waited. "Look Jane see." He pointed at a shooting star. "Quickly. Make a wish."

"I wish tonight would never end!" She said with a deep sigh as she leant on the railings.

Bobby came and stood behind her. He was just wearing his boxers. He slid his arms around her with one hand under her breast and one hand on her belly.

"Did you make a wish too?"

"Of course. Yes." He lent into her ear and whispered softly in his native tongue what his wish was. "Ben bu son vermek ve belki şimdi değil, eğer birgün biz birlikte bir bebek yapabilir istiyorum asla." {I never want this to end and maybe if not now, someday we can make a baby together}

"What does that mean?"

"Someday maybe I will tell you." He kissed the side of her neck.

The sky had started to change from black to grey. Then to purple orange and magenta.

The sun was rising sleepily from is heavenly bed. The colours change every few seconds until she hung high in the sky and all traces of darkness had gone. In the distance they could hear seagulls squawking. The waves lap softly against the side of the boat. They were the only things to be heard apart from her fastening heartbeat that was pounding in her ears. Was this what love felt like?

"Oh Bobby, what a wonderful thing to see. And I got to share it with you. I must say I think this has been the most wonderful night of my life."

"And I think I must say that I think am falling in love with you Janey. I wouldn't have wanted to share this with anyone else."

Jane was a little stunned by the words. How could he love her, they had only had a brief associations. This was supposed to be a bit of fun. A little holiday madness.

"If this is what love is meant feel like, then I must love you too!" The kisses that followed were full of love and hope that maybe it was more than lust. "Oh Bobby, it wasn't supposed to be like this. How can we be together when our lives are worlds apart?"

"If it is meant to be, it will be my Habibi." He kissed her forehead. "We have watched the sun set and a sunrise together. Today I feel like anything is possible."

It sounded also very cheesy but she also knew it to be true.

With that the engines of the cruiser started and the captain shouted to Bugra that they were going to have to make their way into Kusadasi port as the boat was needed for its next day's excursions.

They slipped below and dressed begrudgingly as the tussled sheets look as if they were inviting them back for more. In the galley fridge was filled some fruit and croissants which they took and prepared on the decks little table. She heard the pop of a champagne cork and the fizz if it being poured into glasses. Bobby then topped it off with some orange juice.

"Mimosa?"

"Ooh, yes please." She took a large sip. "Mmmm, yummy." The sun glistened of her now moistened lips. Lips he never wanted to stop kissing.

"Hey! Take it easy we can't take you home tipsy. Lou-Ann is going to string me up as it is, without you going home like a fish in the bottom of a Raki bottle.

"I must say the boat has got enough supplies on board." She looked him square in those gorgeous eyes of his. "You planned to stay out all night, didn't you? How did you know I would?"

"I confess I had hired the boat for the whole night. Just in case you see. A man has to hope that the girl he is falling in love with wants the same as he does. I think that you have answered my question."

"*BUGRA BAHAR*." Jane said with lovable but irritated tone. "You are a presumptuous man, aren't you? And yes, I do want the same as you." They broke into a fit of giggles as he refilled her glass.

They had just finished breakfast as the port came into sight. They sat with his arm around her relaxed and not wanting to go home. What would she tell Lou-Ann. Was Bobby just playing her like Jane had warned? Was his confession of love just a way of getting her back in the sack? But none of that mattered now. Jane loved Bobby Bahar and that was all that mattered right now. The bloody Bahar men were hard not to love!!

CHAPTER 36

Lou-Ann was waiting in the kitchen impatiently for her friends return. She had guessed that they would not return the previous evening as Bobby had discussed his intension with Ahmet and they may not return home until midmorning.

Ahmet had cornered Bobby and told him that Lou-Ann was worried that he would break Jane's heart. So, doing his big brotherly duty he reminded his baby brother to be careful and not to play games with the pretty blonde.

"I have seen the way you are with Jane. Please do not hurt her with your immature games. We all know you like to play around. A different girl every month. You have the interest span of a goldfish. Do don't toy with Jane's affections."

"I am telling you brother, this feels different. It is different. I Promise not to hurt her. She knows how things are and I will not push her into anything she does not want." He sighed and looked like a doe eyed puppy. "I knew when I met her at your wedding that she was special."

"My dearest Bobby, you have got it bad haven't you."

"What will father say? Two of his sons married to English girls. I know he has always wanted me to marry Belina. But I can't. I couldn't, not now."

"Did you say Married? I think you have hit your head or something. This is not my brother speaking." Ahmet laughed at his own sarcasm.

"I did say it. I think I am I love with Jane."

"Do not worry about our father, he will be fine and accept your choice. Eventually, if this is what you wish. Well anyway, I wish you all the very best. I am warning you, do not play her like a violin for your own needs Bobby. Otherwise it will be Lou-Ann's wrath you will have to deal with as well as mine."

"Please do not say anything to father yet. Let's just wait and see where this thing led to for a bit" He begged "and tonight I will know if she feels the same."

Ahmet told Lou-Ann that he warned his little brother to behave and not to play with Jane's affections but he omitted that he used the words love or marriage. He felt it was not his place. It would have taken a blind fool to see that the friendship between them had steadily been getting stronger.

A battered local taxi had bought Jane and Bobby back to the large holiday home. He had not wanted to bother Osman this morning as he had been so kind the day before helping arrange their romantic interlude by the sea. They walked to the back door sheepishly together holding hands as if to make a silent statement. All the residents would know they had been out the whole night and what may have transpired between them. Jane felt slightly embarrassed, she knew Lou-Ann would want all the gory details. Though some were far too erotic to repeat.

"The wondering lovers return at last. I was about to send out a search party." Lou-Ann chuckled. "Thought you might have fallen overboard again." She continued to laugh.

"What is it with you lot, I was constantly reminded yesterday. Bobby kept making sneaky remarks and now you. I think he was more worried about getting his new jacket wet. Mind you at one point there was a distinct possibility I could happen, but I had a handsome hero to catch me." Her cheeks reddened as she looked at her Bobby. "The captain." She said with a twinkle in her eye.

"I assume you two had a good time or did you two argue till dawn?" She asked speculatively but she could tell by the glint in Bobby's eyes and the flushed complexion of her friend that had been a fair amount of other activities going on through the night.

"Argued till dawn." Jane reciprocated.

"I bet you did." Lou-Ann chuffed making her friend pink up again.

Not wanting to disclose the whole events of her evening in full detail she just said how beautiful it was and they had watched the sunrise together. She would save some of the juicier titbits for when they were alone.

"I am starving." Jane declared.

"Me too. Is Zita about?"

"Osman took her to market this morning for some fresh fruit and supplies they should ..." She didn't even get to finish her sentence before Zita came bursting in the back door carrying enough goods to sink a battleship tucked under her arms and laden with bags stuffed to the brim with fresh goods. Shortly after Osman came carrying equally as much. There seemed to be enough to feed the five thousand.

Bobby help her place some bags on the counters

"Tashekular Bobby. You good boy to me. Glad you home safe." She to look curios at the pair as she ruffled his messed-up hair. "I make lunch OK, you two must be hungry. I young once you know. Not always old lady. Food be 20 minutes. Go. Go wash up then food will be done."

Jane flushed with Zita's blatant inference. Halise then came bounding in and nosed in some of the bags with her favourite dolly in hand.

"Halise you wait till lunch, you spoil your apatite little missy."

Zita's English had greatly improved over the last few months now that Lou-Ann was permanent fixture.

Halise looked sulkily to Lou-Ann for her to overrule Zita.

"If you ask nicely you can have a few grapes then you can find Grand Pappa and tell your Pappa that his lunch will be ready soon. He was in the study on the phone to the new London office. Then go check and see if Adam is still sleeping." It would keep her amused for a while as her cousins were out visiting friends for the day.

A small pot of fresh juicy grapes was prepared for the curly haired child before she skipped off to find her Pappa and new baby brother who she doted on and loved him so much. She hoped that someday as sister would come who would love the colour pink as much as she did and play with her dollies and for her to spoil and adore. But for now, she would make do with Adam and all his blue things.

She found her papa in the office as expected on the phone. He had baby Adam on his Knee whilst he was taking his urgent call. But he did not care. He beckoned Halise to come in. She was just big enough to carry the boy so he handed him over so she could take him to his mother for his next feed. She gave Ahmet the message about lunch and went singing back to her stepmother clutching the baby. She found her Grand Pappa sitting on the swinging in the shade on the porch with her Grandmother.

Ahmet enjoyed his stolen moments with his son. Especially the wakeup cuddles. He considered them to be the most precious kind. He would miss them when they went back to Istanbul and back to work.

As promised lunch was prepared in record breaking time with Jane all freshened up, she helped lay the table. The salads were tossed and fresh bread cut and thin slices of grilled chicken. Zita busied herself tirelessly to keep the kitchen organised and clean whilst she was finishing the preparations. The older Brother and his brood would be back later in the day so it was just them for lunch and Bobby's father and mother.

As Bobby's father entered the room, closely followed by his mother he passed a comment in Turkish to Bugra.

"You are a grown man now Bugra." Bobby was holding his breath for he thought he was going to be reprimanded for keeping the pretty little blonde out all night." But you need to show me some respect." His face stern. "If you want to go with this English girl, I give you my blessing but you must not play your usual games. She deserves better. You must choose. Is it Jane or Belina. It is only fair."

Jane did not know what was being said but she guessed the conversation was about her as she had recognised her name.

Bobby let his breath go and stood up and stood next to Jane and in plain spoken English so for all to here and understand he announced

"I choose Jane. Father. I choose Jane!"

Jane quickly became teary eyed by his words. Bobby's father shook his hand. His mother kissed her on both cheeks as if to welcome her to the evergrowing family. Jane found it all quite overwhelming.

The air filled the room with the smell of spicy chicken. Zita pipped up "Come sit, sit. Lunch is getting cold. Eat." With her orders everyone sat and lunch commenced.

Sitting on the same swing on the porch were Halise had found her grandparents, Jane and Bobby sat drinking a glass of wine. This swing seemed to be everyone's favourite place to sit and contemplate life despite being a little old and some threads going in the cushion from constant use. There had been talk of replacing it but no one could bare to see it go. Bobby could see that something was bothering Jane.

"You are very quiet askum. You ok?

"Bobby. When your father was speaking in the kitchen, I understood my name but I thought I heard another woman's name. Who is she?"

"I will not lie to you Jane. It was Belina. My father thought that Belina and I would always marry. She is a very beautiful Turkish girl and is my Father's acquaintance's daughter. She is 24. We have dated several times mainly to please our parents."

"OH! … Do you have feelings for this Belina?" Her heart sunk not wanting to hear the answer.

"Some maybe. I was once infatuated with her. That was along while ago. It was never love. It was always about keeping our parents happy and nothing to do with our own feelings. I kissed her once. It did not feel right. There was no spark. It was like kissing my sister. Metaphorically speaking."

"But your parents still expected you to marry?"

"It would have been good for business. Agreed and arrange marriages still go on. My mother and father's marriage was arranged but they love each other and always have. My mother says she fell in love the day they were introduced. She said he looked a kind man and she took one look at him and fell in love with his eyes."

Jane could do know more than chuckle at Bobby's last comment.

"I know exactly what she means."

"When I go back to Istanbul, I guess I will have to tell her. But I think she will be OK. I do not think she wants to marry me neither. I am more worried about her father, let alone her fearsome mother."

"Lets hope so!" Jane sighed

Jane and Booby spent every waking moment together. There was never a quiet moment with Halise and Adam and there three cousins always running around and playing their childish games. Good old Uncle Bobby was always co-urst into playing a game of football or swimming with them. They hardly left each other side, stealing kisses in the pool and holding hands and at night canoodling on the infamous porch swing. They were like a pair of sausages linked together.

Time was slipping away fast and Jane soon would go back to her mundane life. Back to missing Lou-Ann. And now to add to it missing Bobby too. At least until he could get to visit and god knows when that would be. At least her period came and she would not have to worry about being abandoned with a child should she never see him again.

What would happen when he saw Belina? Would he may be made to marry her?

The rest of the family had still a week to go when she packed to leave. The night before a huge BBQ had been arrange with a few of the Bahar's family friends. It been the turn of the men folk to show off their culinary skills. The woman had been pleasantly surprised at the feast. Even Osman had joined in the fun. Jane tried to stay cheery and positive. She just wanted one more intimate night alone with Bobby so she could declare her true feelings but it was looking increasing less lightly that there would be another night of intense passion.

Just as the sun was about to give everyone one of its glorious sunsets Ahmet shouted for everyone's attention. He thanked his guests for attending. He thanked Jane for coming to their holiday home which hand made his wife very happy.

"I am sure it will not be long before I have to come to London Jane and next time, I shall insist Lou-Ann comes so she can visit with you." Bobby lent into his brother and whispered into his ear.

They nodded in agreement with each other. "Apparently my brother Bobby has something he wants to say."

"Thank-you Ahmet." He looked in the crowd and found Jane's not so pale face and smiled at her. "As you know this summer has been a glorious one. It is always great when the family and friends get together. But I would like to know if this family would accept another member." Jane's mouth popped open aghast. Was he suggesting what she thought? He moved closer to her and Lou-Ann egged her I forward. Bobby dropped to one knee. "My habibi. My Janey. You are an amazing woman I can't now imagine life with you not in it. I am I love with you Jane Berkley. Will you marry me." he tried not to choke on his worlds. He suddenly felt quite overcome with emotion. He slipped his hand in his pocket and pulled out ring pull from a can of cola. Jane just laughed. "It's the best I could do at short notice."

"Oh yes, I will. I love you too." With that she collapsed into his arms with tears free flowing down her face. The family applauded loudly. He slid the ring pull on to her slender finger.

She looked down at the shiny ring pull. She found it quite ironic as bobby's family were exquisite jewellery makers. But in her eyes, it was perfect.

"I promise to replace that as soon as possible with something a little more suitable. You can help design it and I can have whatever you want made."

"It's not the ring that matters, it's what it represents that counts." Holding out her left hand "Maybe I shall ware this forever."

"OK everyone." Ahmet regained everyone's attention." A toast to Jane and Bobby, cheers." The family followed Ahmet's lead a raised their glasses to the newly engaged couple. "Now that's done I have one more announcement to make." Eyes turned to Lou-Ann. Most of the women present thought it would be announcement to say she was having another child. "As most of you know we have just opened a small office in London. And as irritating as it to Lou-Ann I have spent quite a few hours on the telephone negotiating whilst I have been here this summer." He looked at his wife "Sorry Lou-Ann." She smiled a sweet smile of forgiveness. Business was business and sometimes in cut into family time. She understood especially as she knew what the calls were about and it was also for Jane's benefit. "Bobby, I have made it possible for you to go to London and work from the London office so I can have you there to keep an eye on things. And Jane, I trust you will keep an eye on Bobby. This will give you to love birds enough time to see each other and make a happy life together." Ahmet's put his arm around his baby brother with great affection. "And for god's sake brother, A coke ring pull really?" They all laughed together.

CHAPTER 37

The final fond farewells finished, blurred tear filled eyes were dried, Booby threw Jane's bright pink case in the boot of his car. Neither of them ready for their short separation.

As they neared the airport Jane could feel the tears start to rain down her cheeks.

She sniffed and wiped her face. Bobby turned and was also in an unmanly state hiding it behind his sunglasses. Before they knew it, they were standing virtually in the same spot he had picked the blonde from England up just a few short weeks ago. Words would never be enough to quell the bereft feeling in their hearts.

"I love you Jane remember that. It's only for six weeks or so. As soon as the visa are finalised and the office is ready, I shall be with you again. Quicker if I can make it happen." He pulled her to him and wiped the tears from her reddened cheeks.

"Who knew when I stepped of that plane a few weeks ago we would feel like this?"

He put his forehead on hers.

"I think I knew. The moment you stepped out of the arrivals." He smiled at her one of his cheeky grins. "One last kiss, make it a good one this one has to last."

First, he tasted her salty tears on her lips then the kiss became more impassioned, more desperate not wanting it to end. Not caring who saw. Eventually they broke apart for the lack of oxygen. "It's just a few weeks habibi."

"I love you Bobby." She mumbled. "I have to go. God knows I don't want to."

She pecked him briefly on his cheeks. Turned with her bright pink case in tow, then vanished in the crowd and disappeared through passport control.

The next few days at the house Bobby lingered around like a little lost dog until it was time to start packing up to leave. Akin and his wife and three children were the first to leave. Leaving the house leaving the house in a relative state on quietness.

Bobby new when he was back in Istanbul there would be one final hurdle to deal with. He would have to face Belina and her parents. He hoped it would go smoothly and with no big dramas.

Back in London Jane returned to her desk job. She often felt herself daydreaming of their night aboard the little cruiser that Bobby had rented for them. Bobby had certainly new how to satisfy her carnal needs. Needs she didn't even know she had needed quelling. She would just now have to wait impatiently for him to come and satisfy her once more.

CHAPTER 38

Bugra had a thousand things to attend to before departure for his new life and new love in England. When things had been finalised, he would be head of accounting and share some duties in the importing side of things. The Bahar Empire was growing as was its family. Its fine jewellery was about to enter a different market with its unique designs being promoted to wider audience. It long been a dream of Ahmet's to open a London office but his father had always opposed it. He had wanted to concentrate in its high-end market. Not wanting to dilute the quality of its offerings. Now the siblings had the majority control on the business it was now possible. The market was an ever-changing place and it was time to diversify. Ahmet ran most in the company, Akin had his Hotel to run and had agreed to the changes and now the youngest brother was to be placed in London. It was going to make life easier all round. As his ear on the ground, Bobby would report back to his middle brother.

It had been Lou-Ann's idea to install Bobby into his new role. It had been a right place, right time scenario with his romance with Jane blossoming. All they had to do was just hope he would agree to go and of course he had jumped at the chance.

CHAPTER 39

The day had arrived he had been dreading. It was the day he was to tell Belina and her family he did not want to carry on the charade that had been planned for them. It had been decided it would be prudent to have the meeting at Ahmet's house.

Bobby knew in his heart it was the right thing to do and would release Belina and let her find someone she truly loved. He was nervous as their hour of arrival drew closer. What if suddenly caved and agreed? What would happen to his Janey then? He felt some comfort knowing his brothers and family supported his decision. He decided he would not be bullied by Belina father and his decision was final.

The buzzer at the gates went. The gates swung open and the shiny new Mercedes drove up to the heavy wooden front doors. Belina sat in the back with her mother and her father sat next to the capped chauffeur. She was fidgety and nervous. Her mother had made her were a hi-jab covering her long thick black hair. Her mother intended to make her look respectable and suitable marriage material. Belina had been dreading this day as far as she was concerned today would be the day a wedding day was set and her future with Bugra sealed. Belina was as much set against marrying the Bahar boy as he was her. She had heard on the grape vine that he intended to marry an English girl and hope that the rumour was true. But she was sure that her parents had not heard the same or if they had they would try to make him see sense that their precious Belina would make a perfect match as well as being good for business.

Belina's stomach churned as she exited the large Mercedes and entered in the hallway of the Bahar residence. The smell of fresh flowers from the annex floated in the air.

It was Akin and Ahmet that greeted them, Zita closely stood behind offering to take any discarded items they wished to dispose of. The ladies were ushered of to the garden to enjoy the cooler evening air whilst the men went to the lounge were tea would be served and the evenings business would take place. Mr Bahar senior was waiting with a nervous Bobby.

Everyone shook hands hand greeted each other politely like it was a business meeting

"You look like I am about to feed you to the lions, Bugra" Belina's father slapped his back he nearly choked on his tea. "So here we are. Finally, we are to set a date for our children's wedding. I must say, Mrs Emin is more than excited." He took a sip of his own apple tea. "She has already been shopping." He laughed quite jovially.

Mr Bahar senior stood and cleared his throat. He just wanted all his sons to be happy. He now had to try to find the least insulting way of letting them down gently.

"I am afraid your wife's shopping expeditions may have been a bit too premature, my dear friend." Mohammed Emin looked puzzled. "I am afraid our children will not be united in marriage after all."

"WHAT?" He raised his voice. "What are you saying my old friend? This has always been our wish."

"That's exactly my point. A point bought to my attention by Bugra. It is what we that desired, this union, not our children. They deserve the right to choose."

"I can hardly believe what you are saying. Wait until Bilina's Mother finds out, she will be heart broken. Akin please fetch my wife and daughter." He grumbled. "Belina will be devastated."

Akin ushered the ladies in followed by Lou-Ann to stand by her husband. After all this was now *her* home. She wanted to her what was said. After all it concerned her best friend's future.

"After all this time apparently, you will not be marrying Bugra Bahar my dear Belina." She breathed a sigh of visible relief. Tears of disappointment and anger started to show in her mother's eyes. But as a good respectful wife she temporally remained silent. She would get her say later.

Bobby could not keep quiet anymore. He rose to his feet and went to stand at Belina's side in act of unity.

"Mr Emin, Mrs Emin, I am sorry to let your family down but can you not see the pleased reaction on your daughters face. She does not wish to spend her life with me or I her. This agreement you and my father made was never official. It was always assumed. I would not want to be in a loveless marriage, it would not be fair on Belina, she deserves to be truly loved. I have met someone who loves me and who I love so very much and I intend to spend my life with."

Mohammed's nostrils flared angrily. *The cheeky runt* he thought. He felt like his daughter was being rejected, but Belina was determined to have her say without being disrespectful to her father.

"Father please, do not be mad at us. I have never loved Bugra. We have both played along with this charade long enough. It is time to stop." She turned to bobby "I am so very pleased for you Bobby." She turned back to her mother and fathered who were still a little bewildered. "Mother, Father there is someone I would like you to meet. He is a doctor from a good family." Finally, she'd said it and felt all the better for it. "No more lies or secrets. I want to choose my own husband and marry him because I love him not because of some romantic dream my parents had.

Belina's parents looked at their daughter with a mix of admiration and bewilderment. It was her bemused mothers turn to speak.

"A doctor. A surgeon." She naturally elevated his status. "Maybe this will not so bad after all."

Belina was not about to correct her mother and yes, one day he would become a surgeon. A fine one at that. She would correct her mother at a later date when things had settled down. Instead she once again turned to Bobby with a beaming smile relieved in all that had been said.

"Bobby be good to your intended. Do not mess her around." Belina warned him. "She is a lucky lady to have tamed you. I had heard a rumour that you had been caught by cupid's arrow and shunning your girlfriends." She gave a little giggle.

"Jane, her name is Jane." He got a warm fuzzy feeling when he said her name. He long for the day when he could reunite with her at start their life together in his new home in England.

"Well, it seems our children have made their decision." Mohammed sounded somewhat chirpier. His daughter's prospects had recovered and to a '*Surgeon*' no less.

"It seems the younger generation want their own way these days Mohammed. The old ways are dying my dearest friend but who are we to stop from them being happy?"

Mohammed spoke with kindness to his daughter.

"Belina, soon we shall soon make arrangements to meet your Doctor friend and his family. But I also understand there was invitation of dinner this evening." He rubbed his slightly rounded, overweight belly as if to indicate he was hungry. Lou-Ann led the way in an untraditional fashion to the garden were the smell of the wood burning BBQ was waiting with Osman standing proudly next to it ready to cook the meats for the un- engagement feast.

Belina and Bobby walk the garden for a while. She linked arms with him as a friend.

"I was dreading this evening Belina, had had feared that my father would renege on his blessing and make me marry you. I am so pleased you too have found someone." He smiled cheekily at her. "A doctor, I hope he will be good to you?"

"I am sure he will but wait until my mother he is only a junior doctor; she will have kittens. She will get used to the idea I am sure."

"I would love to be a fly on the wall when you tell her." They both laughed out loud and wished each other the very best for the future.

CHAPTER 40

A short while later Jane was reunited with her beloved Bobby in London. It felt like they had been apart for months instead of just weeks.

The first night Bobby arrived, he checked into the same hotel in Knights-bridge that his brother had first clamped eyes on his now wife, Lou-Ann. Jane was nervous about seeing Bobby again. Her stomach flipped with butterflies as she walked through the hotel foyer. She had dressed for the appropriately for the occasion in a beautiful short black dress. Jane had already spotted him at the concierge desk. Her heart raced.

It was as if he had felt her presence. He turned with a big beaming smile as their eyes locked. Time stood still for a short moment. Everyone else seem to vanish and it was just them as they walked with purpose towards each other barley able to contain the passion burning inside them. His lips sealed tightly on hers. Jane thought she was going to explode with love. All her nerves vanished. He was the ONE. Her one and only. The man she thought she would never find. She knew the feelings where reciprocated tenfold and it wasn't just some silly holiday romance.

The Night was long. Making up for lost time they spent the night making love, holding each other and talking about their future.

"Hey Bobby, you never did tell me what you said on the boat".

"It means 'I never want this to end and maybe if not now, someday we can make a baby together.' roughly translated. I knew then I loved you."

"Well if that's the case Mr Bugra Bahar we better get practising!"

With that, they merged their bodies into a single entity one last time before sleep came and took them to a land of peace and love where all dreams come true!!

There life was going to busy preparing for a wedding and searching for a suitable home together in which they could eventually bring up their children and live happily ever after.